Being Normal

Being Normal

Stephen Shieber

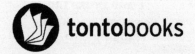 tontobooks

www.tontobooks.com

Published in 2008 by Tonto Books Limited
Copyright © Stephen Shieber 2008
All rights reserved
The moral rights of the author have been asserted

ISBN-13:
9780955632624

British Library Cataloguing in Publication Data:
A catalogue record for this book is available from
the British Library

Printed & bound in Great Britain by
CPI Cox & Wyman, Reading, RG1 8EX

Tonto Books Ltd
Newcastle upon Tyne
United Kingdom

www.tontobooks.com

For everyone who has the courage to
dance to the beat of their own drum.

Contents

Being Normal

My father was a painter and decorator. An artisan, he called himself, in his effusive moments. What he meant was that he slapped up posh wallpapers in houses he quietly lusted after.

He was a man of modest ambition. Towards the end of their marriage, my mother struggled to conceal her contempt. Sometimes, she spat in his tea and stirred it in with a spoon.

'Think that milk's off, Maureen. Me tea's all frothy.'

She moved out the day puberty arrived. I heard the door click shut, but was mesmerised by the ugly bumps on my balls. I didn't get out of the bath, didn't see where she'd gone. She left a note, but it only said that she was off in search of a less normal life. I knew exactly what she meant.

Now there was no one to supervise me while Dad was at work.

'I'll stay here. I promise not to burn the house down.'

He grinned. 'You can come with me. My son. My assistant.'

'I could just stay here...'

My plans for the school holidays included dyeing my hair, experimenting with mascara and memorising the lyrics of The Sisters of Mercy. Helping my father hang the florid wallpapers of snooty suburbanites featured exactly nowhere.

'No. We'll spend some time together lad. Just you and me.'

He winked. I scowled. The matter was settled.

The job was at a hateful terracotta villa, up by the park. When the owner saw my hair, she wrinkled her nose. This took me three hours, Bitch. Marvel at its wonder.

'This is my son, Mrs Goldblatt. My assistant.'

Dad nudged my elbow. I offered my hand, beaming with pride at my ebony fingernails. Mrs Goldblatt declined. I grunted hello. She showed us into the dining room.

'Maybe tomorrow, Son, you'll... tone it down a bit.'

'Maybe.'

Mrs Goldblatt's gilded wheatsheaf chandelier would have sparkled surrounded by blood red walls, but the old trout had chosen a grey paper, foaming with the impossible fractals of monstrous ferns.

Dad complimented her on her excellent taste!

An assistant's job is to clear, fetch and carry. All the while Dad, the artisan, slapped glue onto roughly measured lengths of paper.

'You see, Son, this paper has a huge repeat. Even a small error means we waste a lot. This stuff isn't cheap.'

I stifled a yawn.

'Pass me that brush, Son.'

I passed it.

'Another brew?'

I made it.

'Bag that paper up. A messy workplace equals a messy job.'

Such banal little maxims. I despised them.

On our last day at Mrs Goldblatt's, Dad ran out of razor blades.

'They're essential, my lad, if you want a nice clean edge to the paper.'

'Whatever.'

'Make sure you get my usual brand. Nothing else will do.'

Oh yeah? Every time my father shaved, he ran his hand over his cheeks and stubble grated his calluses.

I set off on my errand, trudging through the park, sun colouring my white face. Every bench I passed I scanned for Mum. Each one was empty. Perhaps she'd jump out from behind a tree and ask me how I was, how Dad was coping without her. Then she'd whisk me away to somewhere exotic and tell me all about her fabulous new life.

Fat chance.

In the chemist's, I got lost among the sanitary towels and other women's things. The assistant, a girl I recognised from school, watched me from behind a large display of condoms. Their bright flashy logos accused me.

'A packet of razor blades, please.'

'Which ones?' She managed to free the question

before it suffocated in her bubble-gum.

I pointed to Dad's brand and she smiled, reaching for them with black talons like my own. The silver eye shadow and black lipstick were cool. Although I thought the floral Alice band jarred against her raven locks.

'Nice look.'

She looked down. 'Thanks. You too.'

Yeah right. I had paint in my hair and wallpaper glue drying on my hands. And Dad's old overalls weren't particularly fashionable.

I handed her a note and she gave me change. For a second, our fingers collided. Chemist Girl smiled at me. I wanted to smile back, but I also wanted to flee. The back of my neck and my armpits were drowned in sweat. I hummed, sweet and stale.

I got to the door.

'You're not going to do yourself in, are you?'

'Pardon?' I looked at her as if she'd farted.

'The razor blades?'

Another jet of perspiration squirted down my back. 'They're for my dad. He decorates houses. Gives a nice clean edge to the paper, apparently.'

'Oh.' She fiddled with her hair and leaned across the counter. Beneath her white coat, her breasts looked like two inflatable pillows, where I might rest my head. I gulped and then she said, 'This is the moment when you ask me out.'

'Is it?'

'Yeah.'

'D'you want... to go out?'

'Maybe.'

'Is that a yes, then?'

'It's a maybe.'

'Oh.'

She blew a huge pink bubble. I waited until it popped and then left.

All the way back to Mrs Goldblatt's our slight conversation replayed in my head. A thousand other ways I could have played it, but I didn't. I couldn't. I doubted I ever would.

'Where've you been?'

'Getting these.' I threw the box at Dad and took pleasure as he fumbled the catch.

'Never mind. Get that mess cleared up. Mrs G'll be back soon.'

I didn't answer. I was a capitalist slave, a ro-bot-of-all-work. For a moment, back there with Chemist Girl, I'd felt human. Dad put me right. Come the revolution, though, the geek and the freak might inherit the earth.

Hands full of scraps, I winced at a sharp, sudden, pain in my thumb. I dropped the rubbish into the bag and examined my offending digit. Watching the bleed was beautiful and exhilarating. A ruby split in my ghostly skin. A clean slice. Not deep, but satisfying. It woke me up.

'What the bugger have you done?' Dad's concern robbed me of my moment. I scowled.

'Bloody hell, Son. Why didn't you check for blades?'

Self-defence wasn't worth it. Dad's negligence

gave me tranquillity. After plastering my wound, I redoubled my efforts, blinded by my revelation. When Mrs Goldblatt returned she paid the fee and gave us a tip. Dad bought us a fish supper and I deigned to eat it with him.

'We make a good team.'

'Yeah.'

Dad hugged me. I froze.

Later, with Dad conked out on Special Brew, I rifled his kit for razor blades, withdrawing one of the unopened packets. Peeling back the waxy paper, I shivered with anticipation. Off came my plaster. An angry line incised my thumb, just below the joint. It looked so bright and perfect. It was, quite simply, beautiful. And it was me.

I thought Chemist Girl was laughing at me. I could imagine her describing me to her mates, laughing over their 20/20, listening to bands I wasn't cool enough to know about, let alone enjoy. At the other end of this summer's evening, my mother was laughing also, grateful she'd escaped the drudgery of family life. Laughing because she'd fooled me so long that she cared.

The steel edge was cold against my arm. It bit cleanly and my flesh quickly wept. One, two, three bloody teardrops. Then a trickle. Then a flow. I lay my head back against the chair and watched, transfixed and transformed.

I never worked for Dad again. There wasn't time. I was my own work of art now. But being beautiful was an expensive business.

'I'm giving you nowt for that stuff. You look like a girl. Where's my son gone?'

'I'll get a job. I'll pay my way.'

'Good luck. Who's going to employ you looking like that?'

Dad had a point. I desperately needed cash.

Traipsing round the fag ends of town, I found my niche in a record shop. So saying, Stigmata Martyr wasn't much of a record shop. There was more dust than vinyl. But Ian wanted an assistant and I needed a job. For this fortuitous coincidence, I thanked the Goddess.

'I don't pay as much as HMV,' said Ian.

'I need enough to keep me in mascara, hair dye and fishnets.' Fishnets that I hacked into sleeves, my scars camouflaged by their weave.

'Can you start Saturday?'

'This Saturday?'

He nodded.

'See you at nine?'

Ian yawned. 'Oh, ten at the earliest, please.'

I laughed and went home to break the news. Dad examined his hands and muttered something that sounded like he was proud of me.

Saturday came and I appeared at the door of Stigmata Martyr in full Geisha make-up. Eyebrows severely plucked, corpse-white mask and crimson lips – a mixture of No 7 and my own blood. After Ian's initial shock, he smiled and opened the door.

'You look amazing.'

'You think so?'

'Beautiful. Cool, little brother.'

For the first time in months, I smiled and meant it. That first shift passed slowly, but soon word got around that Stigmata Martyr had a new attraction. Me. Customers wandered in and, even if they found nothing to buy from our paltry stock, they stayed to gaze at Geisha Boy. My scars burned beneath my sleeves, but I was happy.

Ian was happy too. 'Sales have gone up since I took you on,' he told me over a cup of rosehip tea one Saturday evening.

'By how much?' My vanity was curious.

Ian shivered. 'Ugh, maths and things. They've gone up, that's all.'

In the end, it was enough to know that I was admired.

One Saturday, Chemist Girl appeared. By then, Geisha Boy was back in the make-up bag. After all, my fans needed more than just one look. So, that day, I was Struwwelpeter crossed with Edward Scissorhands. I'd risen at five to blow-dry and set my hair.

'Can I help you, Madam?'

I stood triumphant behind my counter. Behind my makeup. I directed her to the single she wanted and watched as she browsed the racks. Her look hadn't changed. I wished she'd made the effort.

'That's 1.99,' I said to Chemist Girl, looking her

up and down with a scowl. She folded her arms across her crocheted top, restraining those incredible breasts of hers. A huge silver ankh around her neck jangled on its chain and glinted.

'It's you, isn't it?'

'Who?' I shrugged, trying to preserve my fragile nonchalance.

I handed over her bagged single and she took it, looking me up and down.

'Your dad's decorating business must be doing well.'

'What?'

'The amount of blades you buy.'

Tears pricked my eyes. Stigmata Martyr blurred.

She watched as I rubbed my arm and then shook her head. 'Ask me out again when you've sorted yourself out.'

The door banged behind her, leaving me alone. I pushed my way through the bright strips of plastic that curtained off Ian's den from the shop. Through there, I let go.

'Hey, what's the matter?'

Ian appeared from nowhere and, before I knew it, his arms braced my back. His shoulder was convenient for my head. My whole body vibrated. My snot dried on his jumper.

'Come on. It can't be that bad. I'll change the tape. Joy Division does this to some people.'

I looked up at him. Then I bared my arms and held them up for his inspection.

'Oh. Oh,' he said, drifting into babble mode.

'This is heavy shit. Seriously heavy shit. But cool, man. Cool, little brother.'

I reached around to the pocket of my black, skinny-fit Levi's. But I'd left my blades at home. It was all I could do not to scream.

'Sit down. I'll make you some camomile.'

It tasted of old ladies' perfume, and possibly their wee, but I sipped it anyway, rather than refuse a badly-needed kindness. The mirror on the table reflected a tragic creature. Below my smeared eyes, thick drops of mascara clumped on my cheeks. My lips faded to dun. I ran my tongue over them, tasting the faint metallic tang of my blood.

I eyed the mirror. It could cut me more deeply than I usually dared. It was the obvious way out of my misery, the walking disaster that was my life.

'Why?'

I shrugged. No one had asked me this before, because I'd told no one. They wouldn't understand. It was power. Beauty. Release.

'It helps.'

'There are other ways, you know.'

Tell me them.

'Look at you. You're marvellous. You're beautiful.'

I laughed. The mirror told a different story.

'Okay, not at the moment, perhaps. But you are. Wait here a minute.'

I didn't want to be left, but desperation deadened my tongue. I looked at the mirror again. It

18

wouldn't take much to smash it. I closed my eyes and anticipated the moment, the divine release.

Yet something stopped me. I sat in that cramped little kitchen, with its Formica table and lingering dope smell and thanked the Goddess for Ian's kindness. I could hardly repay him with a trip to casualty. If I took the mirror now, I wouldn't be able to stop cutting. Not until I'd carved all the pain away.

Ian stood in the doorway watching me. I turned to face him and he flashed me a brilliant smile. It didn't work a miracle, but it helped.

He looked at his watch. 'No point in opening up again today.'

'Isn't there?'

'Fancy a sandwich? Or a walk?'

I looked at myself through my father's eyes, through my mother's, through Chemist Girl's eyes and shook my head.

'Not like this.'

'Here. Use these.'

He tossed me a packet of facial wipes. I took a handful of them and murdered Struwwelpeter. I cleansed myself of Edward Scissorhands and erased Geisha Boy. There I sat, examining my disappointing, denuded face, when Ian appeared in the mirror behind me. It was easier to study him.

'What you looking at,' Ian asked, eyes avoiding mine.

'You.'

'Why?'

Why? He was an ordinary bloke. He wore no makeup, except for a trace of mascara. He didn't blow-dry his sandy hair. He could face the world without all that. And he was kind.

'You're nice, Ian. That's all.'

He didn't answer, except in the form of a shrug. I balled the clogged wipes together and aimed them at the bin. Ian applauded my shot.

'There. You're done. Let's go.'

I held out my arms again.

'Oh, of course. I'll get you a jumper.'

He bounded off. Once more to the rescue.

More sunlight. This really wouldn't do for my maudlin self. But it was a short walk to the sandwich shop and we talked like friends, without touching on the things that hurt. At the yellow door, I hesitated, allowing Ian to show me the way.

On the wall, behind the counter, hung three large blackboards, patiently inscribed with a bewildering set of choices. Ten varieties of bread, twenty varieties of sandwich filling. I studied them all until I felt dizzy and then asked for a ham and pease pudding stottie.

'Does it get any easier,' I asked my boss, as we waited for our lunches.

'What? Choosing sandwiches? I dunno. I tend to get the same thing each time – hummus and veg.'

'No – "It".'

He was playing me. I wanted to laugh and I

wanted to punch him in the arm. This was serious. I was serious. God, I was so tired of being serious.

'What "It"? Selling records?'

'No, IT! Girls? Life? Happiness? '

Ian considered my question for a long time, running a hand through his hair and raising his eyes to the ceiling. Above our heads a fan whirred, filling his silence. Then he looked at me and, in answer, smiled again and shrugged.

The Good Little Wife

Kate checks the details once more and then spirits the train ticket away into the inner pocket of her handbag, along with her credit card. She could have saved herself the prolonged excursion to the travel centre, but booking on-line felt like a cheat. A reference number is no substitute for a cardboard ticket.

She walks out of the station and gets into the car. On the back seat is today's shopping. Kate reads through Andrew's list again. Salmon. Star anise. Cinnamon sticks. Melon. Parma ham. Wine. Gin. All present, all correct. Just as he requested.

Andrew will be pleased.

She crumples up the shopping list and drops it into the ashtray, zooming off to her next call.

The girl in the dry cleaner's is indifferent to Kate. She greets her with the practised half-smile of a customer care course. Kate sighs and reaches for her plastic-bagged items. The two women brush against each other and Kate immediately shrinks back, draws herself in and shivers.

'Thank you'.

She cannot disguise her wavering voice. She slopes back to the car, avoiding embarrassment.

On the way home, she passes the primary school. The younger children are being collected for their lunch. She recognises one or two of the stay-at-home mothers, women she once counted as friends. For a while, perhaps these women kept her a place at the school gates. They assumed that she would join them in the heady round of school runs and party runs. Perhaps they imagined shared trips to bowling alleys, swimming pools and pizza parlours.

Kate stares straight ahead and accelerates, so that no one has to feel awkward on her account.

At home, she places the salmon steaks into a roasting tray, drowning them in white wine. She scatters the spices over them, still uncertain why her husband asked for salmon. Such a bland fish always needs something to make excuses for it.

But Andrew knows best.

Kate takes a slug from the open wine.

Melon balls splat on the floor. Kate comes to her senses, angry at the mess she's made. Tonight must be perfect for the boss and his wife. A promotion is in the offing.

And I deserve this, Katherine, I really do.

The afternoon passes quickly – arranging the flowers, folding napkins, painstakingly creating the canapés. Everything looks just right, just as she planned it. Satisfied, Kate wipes her hands on a tea towel (something Andrew hates her doing) and takes a peek in her handbag.

Yes, the ticket is still there. She flips the folder open and checks all the details again. When she's finally away, she doesn't know what she will do. It will be enough to step down to the platform, knowing she has disappeared, knowing that he cannot find her.

Kate runs a bath. She lowers herself carefully into the scalding water. It bites and pinches her skin, turning her pink. She gasps and squirms until the dull burning matches the pain in her ribs.

Fixed to her dressing table mirror is Andrew's 'last minute' list. Fill ice bucket. Remove canapés from fridge. Smile. Be charming. Obedient.

Kate snatches this final list down and shreds it. She places the pieces in her bin and sets light to them. They glow briefly and then turn to ashes.

Drying her hair, Kate smiles at her reflection. She's learnt to play Andrew at his own game, using his guilt to gain her all the material comfort she can stomach.

She feels vague ingratitude for throwing it away. But she's hungry for something less likely to fail. The Mercedes' engine has a recurring fault and she's getting to the age where aiming to be fashionable is unseemly.

The door opens behind her and Kate starts up.

'Hello darling.' He grazes her cheek with his lips, casting an appraising eye over her body. Ever since this dinner party was first mooted, Andrew has been sparing in his attentions. Kate has no bruises above the tops of her breasts.

'Show me the dress.'

'I'm not ready yet, Andrew. Later.'

His left foot taps against the bedroom floor.

'Show me the dress, Katherine.'

Kate stamps down her rebellious urges, the desire to throw it all away. To slap him in the face with her credit card and train ticket. She drops her robe, treating him to an eyeful of his handiwork. She is slow to pull on her knickers and stockings.

'No bra?'

Kate smiles. 'Not in that.'

Andrew pulls her dress off its hanger and gathers it in a bunch over her head, waiting for her to raise her arms. Kate resists the urge to wince as her ribs ring with pain. She smoothes herself down and steps into her heels.

'Jewellery?'

She hasn't prepared for this. Panic clutches her stomach.

'The pearls?'

Andrew waits. Kate gropes for the correct answer, but Andrew breaks the silence first.

'If you want to wear the pearls, Katherine, you go ahead. Why make a special effort for me?'

She wants to sink her fingernails into his fleshy cheeks, until he squeals like a pig. Until blood flows down his face.

'What about the emerald necklace, darling?'

Kate searches her jewellery box. 'Yes, yes of course.' Why didn't she think of it before? The emerald was expensive. She could pawn it.

She extracts the necklace and lets Andrew fasten it for her. His breath tingles on her neck. Kate freezes, until he moves aside.

'Hair up or hair down?'

'Hair up, of course, Katherine.' Andrew hands her a jewelled clip and the silver brush from the set he bought her last Christmas. Kate watches in the mirror as he undresses.

The kitchen knife would slide easily through his flabby white torso, blood staining the greying ladder of hairs between his chest and navel. Sighing, Kate rises from the stool and excuses herself, muttering about checking the salmon.

'But what about my back? I need my back soaping.'

The air ignites. 'Andrew, darling,' she begins, not convinced she has the strength to continue. Her tongue may flop, limp and useless, before the words are out. 'Andrew. Just see to yourself, for once.'

'What?'

'If you like, I can tell Mr and Mrs Lennon that dinner is ruined because I had to pull you off.'

Thunderclouds eclipse his face. Kate crosses the room, witness to her own bold display. She kisses him on the cheek and takes hold of his right hand, cupping it against his crotch.

'God gave you hands for a reason. Put this one to good use.'

She leaves the room without waiting for his response.

The guests arrive at eight o'clock. Andrew mixes Martinis, polishes the glasses and tips the olives into a bowl.

Kate checks herself in the hall mirror before she opens the door. Should she let the top of her dress slip a little? Will they notice the tooth marks on her breasts? Perhaps if she takes the emerald off...

'Mr and Mrs Lennon. Lovely to see you.'

Kate steps back to let them in, feeling Andrew's arm encircling her waist. His weight and height offer her a moment's security; transport her back to happier days. A wave of love for him surprises her, but their days as a real couple are long over. Kate struggles to retain her balance and falls back into Andrew, crumpling his suit. He lifts her like a feather, setting her down in the direction of the kitchen.

Oh yes, the canapés... the performance of her life.

Kate lifts the tray and pushes open the kitchen door with her free hand. The sitting room is filled with the false laughter and polite conversation that is the currency of their marriage. Making sure her own smile hasn't slipped, Kate offers the tray to Mr and Mrs Lennon. She is aware that the oven needs turning down.

Mr Lennon wipes his dry, puckered mouth and turns his attention to Kate.

'So, my dear, how would you feel if Andrew was promoted? It would mean a lot more time away from home. And I'm afraid the expense account wouldn't stretch to you accompanying him all the time.'

Kate mentally scans the good wife script to find her line but, before she can speak, Andrew jumps in.

'Katherine's utterly supportive of my career. Aren't you, darling? She's very good like that. And she certainly benefits...'

He gestures to the room around them. Lennon coughs. Kate blushes.

'Actually, Mr Lennon, Mrs Lennon, I wanted to talk to you about Andrew's promotion.'

'You do?' asks Mrs Lennon.

Kate flicks a glance at Andrew, whose face mirrors the old woman's concern. This is it. Her moment. Everything else has led to this. All she has to do is step out of the shadows.

Trembling, Kate rises, unzips and wriggles out of the black shell of her dress. She submits herself to Mr and Mrs Lennon's scrutiny, feels positively pornographic as the old couple shuffle forward in their seats.

Time comes to a standstill. Kate watches her little cabaret from somewhere outside herself.

She lifts her arms to display her husband's bites on her breasts, lets them see how her white skin is pocked and scarred. She feels Andrew's shadow fall on her, hears his voice as if underwater, and smells the charring fish. Her burning skin is cooled by the frozen gasps of Mr and Mrs Lennon. Two pairs of eyes scan the garland of livid bruises adorning her torso. Satisfied, Kate turns around and rolls down her stockings so they can fully appreciate the damage a cigarette end can do. Andrew only smokes for this very purpose.

But the silence is awful. She begins to sing, to fill the yawning void in her lounge.

'I feel pretty, oh so pretty...'

Above her song, Andrew roars. Mrs Lennon stumbles forward, grabbing up the discarded dress and using it to shield Kate's breasts. Kate shudders and moans.

The men's strong arms encircle her and lift her up.

There will be a fire if someone doesn't turn off the oven soon.

Mrs Lennon rushes down the hall to the kitchen as the men carry Kate upstairs. The world lurches and rotates and she wants to vomit. They hold her too tightly. She lets her body go limp in their grasp.

As the Lennons shuffle out the door, Kate hears them reassure her husband that all will be well. That there are therapies, possible cures, for problems such as hers. That they'll do anything they can to support him but, for now, his wife's mental health must come first.

The front door shuts and Kate squirms. She waits for Andrew to return, reading her script again, more than familiar with the next scene.

The back of his hand strikes her face. His knuckles bruise her cheek.

Tomorrow, she will hand over that credit card and train ticket to Andrew. Tomorrow, she'll return to being a good little wife.

Sunday Lunch

O nce again, we've gathered in the family nest. It's a monthly thing, much dreaded. Only, today is far, far worse. Today, I have a plan.

To my left is Dan's brother, Ashley, spearing slices of beef with his fork and swallowing them whole. A Neanderthal who, in other circumstances... well, let's just say that he fills out his Fred Perry t-shirt very nicely.

Ash is a sanitaryware salesman. He spends his life talking shit.

On his other side is Honey, his wife, tousling a strand of her backcombed bleached-to-within-an-inch-of-white hair between two sharply manicured talons. They're in the squoval style – squared ovals – the next big trend in nails, apparently. She hardly fills her boob tube, but it seems cruel to point this out.

For once, I'm sat next to Dan, so Pamela must believe we can get through a meal without fondling each other at the table. Finally, she might be ready to accept that her darling youngest son is corruptor as much as corrupted. Still, the Ice Maiden's keeping one eye on us from her end of the table. Her other eye is glued to Vic's wineglass.

I'm close to screaming pitch. Maybe I'll just fall through a gap in the cabbage roses on the wall and never be seen again.

Thankfully, Paris and Venice, Pamela and Vic's platinum-headed grandchildren, have been banished to the garden. Otherwise, I'd be out the door without opening it.

I need to get a grip and remember that I'm on a mission.

Pamela steeples her fingers under her collapsing chin. She and Honey visit the nail-bar together, a bonding session that, of course, I'm never invited to. Pamela's nails are non-squoval. Neither are they blood red, like Honey's. Pamela's a French manicure sort of woman.

'That beef is excellent, if I say so myself.'

Honey smiles at her mother-in-law. Ash mumbles, his mouth so full that gravy dribbles from the corners.

I sigh loudly, in preparation for my moment.

Dan turns to me, 'What's up with you?'

'Nothing,' I say, giving him my sweetest smile.

'Something wrong Daniel? Alan?'

'No, Pamela, thank you.' I rise, holding onto the table, having never felt so unsteady on my feet in my life. 'I just want to say something.'

'Al, sit down and finish your dinner.'

'No, I have something important to say.'

My lover is the colour of fine porcelain. Beads of sweat shine in his hairline. I find his furrowed brow and jutting chin impossibly cute.

Pamela interjects. 'Daniel, don't be rude. Let

Alan speak. He knows us well enough by now.'

Dan drowns his protests in Rioja. Across the table, his father mirrors him. I scan Dan's face for tell-tale broken veins.

'Thank you, Pamela. I'm glad that we're all here. I can't think of anywhere else I would rather say this.'

'Whatever this is, does it have to be now?'

Now or in a few weeks time, Dan, I suspect the outcome will be the same. Of course, I could back out; compliment Pamela on another excellent lunch and sit back down, without having rocked the boat. But I'm not like that.

Ash drops his cutlery onto his plate. Pamela shoots a protective glance at her disrespected hand-painted china. Hyacinth Bucket owns a similar service.

Dan rises. 'Anyone for more wine? I need more wine. Dad, you'll have some won't you?'

Of course Vic'll have some; he's the living embodiment of Brewer's Droop! He's spent the last twenty years sozzled and flaccid. No wonder Pamela has a permanent pout.

'Dan, hurry back, please. This is about you.'

He takes no notice, but disappears in search of liquid courage. I could do with some myself.

Honey rises also, draping her arm across Ash's shoulders as she goes. 'I'll check on the twins.'

She trots across the oak flooring, her stilettos causing mass destruction. Pamela winces. I'm sure only I see her pain.

'Well I must say, Alan, you've got us all

intrigued. We're on tenterhooks here. Aren't we, Pammy?'

She shrugs Vic off, her eyes narrow and feline. 'Quite.'

'Dan and Honey'll be back in a minute. Then I'll reveal all.'

If Pamela's face gets any tighter, it'll crack.

'Do you want Paris and Venice here as well?' Ash is back with us. 'Only I can tell Honey...'

I wave a hand in dismissal. 'No, no. Don't interrupt whatever they're doing. They'll hear about it later.'

'Oh.'

I drum out the passing seconds on the edge of the table. A cord tightens in Pamela's turkey neck. Vic cradles his empty glass. His nose radiates.

Honey clatters back to us and re-seats herself.

'Is next door's cat black and white, Pamela?'

'Yes dear. Why?'

'The kids were... playing with it, that's all.'

'Well, should they be, dear?'

Honey ponders for a moment. I want to put her out of her misery.

'Cats move quite fast, don't they? It should be okay.'

Pamela adjusts her pearls, craning her neck to catch a glimpse of the delinquents through the window. She won't leave the table for a proper look. She's not the interfering kind of mother-in-law.

Dan returns with the new bottle of wine. His

face has collapsed into the hangdog look he wears whenever he has to visit the dentist or the doctor. I feel equal amounts of love and contempt for him.

He can't look at me. His hand trembles as he refreshes wineglasses.

When he sits back down, I strike.

'Daniel...' I sink down to one knee. If I'm going to do it, I might as well do it properly.

Honey squeals. Pamela sucks in air like a drowning woman. Dan covers his face with his right hand, as I reach for his left.

'...Would you do me the honour of being my civil partner?'

There is silence. Pure, thick silence, which someone's going to have to use a chainsaw to cut through.

Honey squeals again. 'Oh, I can't bear it. Give him an answer, Dan.'

Ash joins my cheerleading team. 'Yes, go on, Bro. Tell him yes.'

Pamela and Vic look on, like car-crash observers.

'Go on, Daniel, give Alan an answer.'

This is a mistake. A huge fat, glowing mistake. Dan looks like he's about to cry. He has the flushed cheeks of a teething baby. I just want to hold him, but he shoves his way past my outstretched arms, knocking over the last of his wine in the process.

At least I haven't bought him a sparkling engagement ring. At least I'm not that tacky.

Pamela's lips narrow to a single line. She gives

an equine snort and fixes me with a look of utter contempt, tinged with self-congratulation.

'You want to take the plunge with my brother, then, Alan?' Ash grabs Honey's hand and squeezes it. 'Best thing I ever did.' Honey shoots him a look of uncomprehending adoration. They're so well suited to each other.

'Well, of course, it's not a marriage really, Ash. That sort of thing isn't allowed for people like us. But I thought... I hoped that we were ready to commit to each other permanently.'

I turn my gaze to the dining room door, hoping Dan will re-appear, smiling and accepting my proposal. Somebody needs to do something; otherwise we might never be able to leave these seats again.

Vic chuckles. 'Why the grand gesture, Alan? You boys already have a mortgage. Marriage is just one more hassle, isn't it Pammy?'

I think my possible future mother-in-law may well swallow her own lips.

Vic squashes her into a hug and smacks a kiss on her cheek.

'Get off. I think you've had more than enough.'

'If only Pammy. If only...'

Vic cracks up over his joke. The rest of us look down at our plates, or at the William Morris table linen. When Vic stops laughing, he's the colour of raw liver.

'Ahhh! My ball and chain. Thirty-five years and counting. Isn't that right, Pammy? My son would be a fool to turn you down, Alan.'

'Thank you very much, Vic.'

Dan still doesn't return.

'I think the surprise might have been too much for him. Maybe I should check he's okay...'

I rise, but Pamela raises her hand, forbidding me to leave. She's also turned violently pale.

'Alan, I think you should leave him alone.'

I want to protest, but I know better. Ash picks at his teeth. Honey teases out a strand of hair, lost in thoughtless contemplation. Vic reaches for the Rioja. Pamela rises, gathering up plates as she goes.

'Of course, I never voted for a Labour government,' she says, as she leaves the room.

'You still haven't given me an answer.'

Dan doesn't respond. He hasn't spoken to me since lunch. I wind down the window and take deep gulps of air. Petrol fumes scour my throat.

Every third Sunday of the month we go to Vic and Pamela's. I count down the days until the call, until once more the summons is issued in those fake bright tones.

'It would be lovely, Alan, if you and Dan could join us for lunch on Sunday.'

And each time, I find myself answering in an equally bright, equally false voice, 'Our pleasure, Pamela.'

I've tried reciprocating, but Pamela doesn't visit. She doesn't 'do' other people's Sunday lunches. She doesn't 'do' anyone else's life but her own. And I think my Dan is the same.

The proposal? God knows I love Dan, but perhaps it's just to prove a point. God forbid that we should actually admit to his family, the rest of the world, or ourselves that we have something going on here.

'What the hell do you think you were doing, Alan? Asking me to marry you? In front of my parents? She was absolutely... mortified. I... was absolutely mortified.'

'Would it help if I apologised?'

Dan replies by stamping on the accelerator. I cling to the dashboard, my knuckles blanching.

Back home, Dan stomps into our bedroom, slamming the door behind him. I pour myself a gin. The bedroom door flies open. A pillow sails through the air and lands at my feet.

'I take it I can't have two?'

'Only if you get it yourself.'

'What about a quilt?'

It lands next to the pillow a second later.

'A goodnight kiss?'

The door slams shut. I pour myself another gin and make up a huffy bed on the sofa.

'Night, Dan.' Of course, he doesn't respond.

'You still haven't given me an answer,' I whisper into the darkened room. Draining my gin, I worm under the quilt, close my eyes and comfort myself with the thought that, if nothing else comes of today, I probably won't ever have to eat off that hand-painted dinner service again.

Sour Milk

Six months after their marriage, Deborah wakes to find herself in bed with Leo. It's a novelty she's not all that happy with. Usually his insomnia and her distaste keep them apart.

Her chin is flattened against his chest and the hair that forests his upper body tickles her nostrils. His right arm is a tube of uncooked pastry. She wishes she'd convinced him to spend longer in the gym, to visit her tanning salon more often. The smell of Leo on her skin makes Deborah nauseous.

Deborah swallows air and winces, because her throat is lined with needle-sharp blades after several glasses of wine too many. So many glasses of wine needed to convince her to end up here.

Deborah's always considered marriage such a petty institution. But Leo turned his salesman charm on her, conjuring up visions of taffeta and platinum and, beyond the wedding day, a life of security and ease.

She's always known it would never work.

Rolling out from under him, Deborah digs her elbow into Leo's ribs. He groans and rolls over.

'We need to talk.' The nausea subsides, but the feeling of wrongness remains. They're both actors, playing at being married. What Deborah needs is to find some authenticity.

Leo yawns, revealing his gold filings, and says, 'We need a lie-in.' He tries to pull her back into him, but Deborah plays dead and resists his embrace.

'What do you want to talk about?' He yawns and then scratches his chest.

'Not here.' She can't be in this bed with him, not as he is, this great lump of flesh, this otherness.

Leo raises himself on one arm and squints at her. 'Where then, Deb?'

'In the kitchen. Over breakfast.' She won't eat. She can't. But Deborah knows it's certain to rouse him. She slips out from under the quilt and sets off for the kitchen, leaving him to follow.

Deborah throttles the oranges with extra vigour and places two full glasses on the table, while Leo warms some bagels for them both. He sets one down in front of her, despite her protests.

Then he leans across to kiss her. Again, she tenses up.

'What's wrong?' His large brown eyes are full of sympathy, but it doesn't touch her. It's as if there's an invisible wall thrown up between them, leaving her alone with her store of revulsion and him with his unknowing optimism.

'I don't think we can go on, Leo. Not like this. We live separate lives. We don't have sex any more. '

'We did last night.'

'Last night was a hiccup.'

She watches his shoulders drop. Cruelty tastes like bile in her mouth. But she's certain about this. As certain as she can be.

'Is there someone else?'

Deborah shakes her head, surprised at the hurt in Leo's voice.

'Then what is it?'

'It doesn't work,' she explains with some exasperation 'we don't work. That's why I think you should leave.'

Leo doesn't answer straight away. Deborah's certain he's punishing her, making her wait until she is tempted to take these words back, to rise from the table and go on with the new day as if none of her feelings have happened.

'Whatever it is, I can change. I know I can be whatever you want... need me to be.'

Deborah laughs. 'Don't be ridiculous. It isn't about you changing. Some things aren't meant to work. We're one of them.'

Leo puts down the remaining quarter of his bagel and leans across the table. It's like he's turning a searchlight on her, or one of those horribly bright interrogation lamps used by the arresting officers in crime films. Deborah's instinct is to examine the weave of the tablecloth, but she takes a deep breath and stares right back at him, determined not to be cowed.

Eventually, Leo asks, 'Why do I have to go?'

'Well, I can't, can I?' Deborah downs her orange juice and rises from the table. 'Let's not argue about this, Leo. You can always go to your mother's. Say... next week?'

She believes break-ups should be swift and neat. Put the knife to a relationship's throat and make one clean cut. Or, if you prefer, a brief, powerful thrust to its heart. There's no need to remain behind, listening to life hiss away.

Apportioning blame leaves people sore. It's sadistic. Listing all the reasons why things have gone wrong is plain masochism. Love might be a battlefield, but Deborah doesn't believe there's any need to rub salt into the wounds.

So she does her best, over the next week, to convince her husband that his leaving the marital home is the only way forward. She stops ironing his shirts, moves him into the spare room and refuses to let him watch the evening news, because she is watching an awful talk show, full of dreadful, common people with tawdry lives. The sort of thing she left behind years ago. She also 'loses' her wedding ring down the waste disposal.

Leo lives through all this with the silent forbearance of the martyr. It's no surprise then, that she finds him in the kitchen a week later, grilling mackerel for them both and opening a bottle of chardonnay.

'You were meant to be gone by today.'

'Sit down and have some dinner. Enjoy a glass of wine. Then we'll talk about our future together. Or apart.'

She looks at him hopefully while she slugs down half her wine. 'You're going to leave?'

'I didn't say that.'

'Go on Leo. Please. Make this easier on both of us. Move out.'

He looks at her as if she's just shot his puppy.

'Wouldn't you like a flat of your own, Deb? Somewhere you can please yourself.'

'I want this house. You could go to your mother's. Or to your ex-wife's. I'm sure she'd love to see you back.'

Leo puts down his fork and reaches for Deborah's hand. 'It's you I want, Deb. Why d'you think I left her?'

'You tell me, Leo. Anyway, I just feel that it's...'

'Feel. Feel. Feel. Honestly, it this was just about feelings, I would've walked out ages ago.'

'What d'you mean?'

Leo looks back down at his food. Now he's avoiding her gaze.

'Marriage is about more than feelings, Deb.'

Her eyes are sore. He's irritating her with his need to be right, with his sanctimonious certainty.

'I don't want to be married to you, Leo.'

'But I still want to be married to you, Deb. Deborah...'

Deborah sighs. She wonders if it's worth staying, or whether she should go upstairs, pack some bags and leave. It would solve one problem. And the house isn't great. It's only three floors and there's no hope of building the basement kitchen she's always wanted, but she can't face starting again. The market being what it is, falling off the property ladder might break all her financial bones. She might even have to get a job. Or go back to the old one.

They both push aside their plates and reach for the wine bottle. Another glass down and, with neither of them moving, Deborah says, 'What would it take, Leo?'

'What would what take?'

'What would it take for you to fall out of love with me?'

Leo clears the plates and takes them to the sink. 'It's not going to happen, Deb. I'm not going to make the same mistakes again.'

We'll see about that, thinks Deborah, as she excuses herself and makes her way up to the spare room.

A week of exile in here and Leo has nested. By his bed is the latest stack of crime novels. He's addicted and buys at least ten each month. His excuse is that they ease his insomnia.

Deborah stares at her husband's tower of murderous words with black hatred. She swears that these are the cause of his insomnia, not its solution. And the reason they've spent so many nights apart. On impulse, Deborah takes each novel from the pile, rips out the last page and then replaces it as if nothing has happened.

'Hi Deb. Come to make up?'

They meet on the landing, Deborah hastily balling her paper crop into her fist.

'Fat chance.'

Leo leans to kiss her, but she ducks out of his way, fleeing down the stairs.

In his office, she starts up the shredder and

chuckles to herself.

This is just the beginning.

Breakfast is fun. Leo appears, yawning furiously.

'Bad night?' Deborah fights to keep the glee from her voice.

'You know – my insomnia again. And it was so hot last night. Did you leave the heating on?'

'Maybe.'

'And – to top it all – for some reason, my book's last page was missing. You know how I hate not finding out who did what.' Leo looks at her archly.

What's he expecting? Confession? Contrition? Fool! This is a war that she intends to win.

'In fact, none of my books had their last pages.'

'Tsk-tsk. Publishers these days. Still, I suppose it's a way of keeping you interested.'

Leo shrugs. 'I suppose.'

Deborah hands Leo the jug of milk that's been sitting above the kitchen radiator all night and flicks through her celebrity magazine with her feet crossed on the table.

Leo eats in silence, but Deborah enjoys his grimace as the milk hits his tongue. She waits for him to complain, but Leo finishes his bran, rises from the table, kisses her on the top of the head and picks up his briefcase. All the while he's humming something, though it's hard to say what. It's not his usual classical rubbish, that's for sure.

It's only when he slams the front door behind him that she realises what the music is. Tears prick her eyes as she recalls how she'd conned herself into being hopeful on the day of their wedding. She retreats to the safety of her bed, hugging herself, amazed at the tyranny of the human heart.

Deborah spends the morning carting Leo's reference library up to the charity shop on the high street. She clears three hundred volumes, so that she can fill the empty shelves with as many ornaments as she can buy.

He hates ornaments. Calls them 'dust-catchers'. Deborah just wants to have some stuff of her own in a house that is furnished with the cast-offs from Leo's previous life.

The glass clowns are hideous, a cross between children's drawings and something more sinister. What Deborah particularly hates is their garish colours, as if each figure has been modelled from e-numbered boiled sweets. Still, the set came cheap from the same charity shop that took the books. And if she hates them, she can only begin to imagine Leo's rage.

She is in the kitchen, fixing gins like nothing has happened, when Leo appears. To her consternation, he is beaming.

'I'd almost forgotten those clowns existed. My grandmother collected them. A new one every time she went to Venice. I used to love them.'

Deborah hands him a gin and admires her husband's control. Leo kisses her on the cheek.

'So thoughtful of you. Where did you get them?'

Her own rage is not so easily concealed, so

Deborah simply shrugs.

'Doesn't matter. I'm just so thrilled to have them.'

Deborah takes a swig of gin. 'What about your books? I gave them to the charity shop.'

He studies her for a moment or two and then tastes his gin. 'Did you?' Leo sighs and Deborah waits for the explosion.

'Are you angry? Do you hate me?'

Leo shakes his head. 'Not at all. It's a relief, being freed from all those unread words. All that knowledge that I'll never use.'

Deborah turns the oven up to its highest setting. 'Give it another 45 minutes, Leo, and your dinner will be ready.' She collects the gin bottle and her glass and carries them upstairs. Some time later, she hears the smoke alarm go off and Leo swear as he tries to rescue his food from the oven.

The next morning, Deborah is confronted with the hideous, lopsided cheerfulness of her clown collection. She tries to ignore their garishness as she plots. What does her husband love more than words?

Of course! His music! A massive CD collection that she remembers watching him painstakingly alphabetise on the racks in the dining room.

Having failed to wound him with the grand gesture of the clowns, Deborah opts for subtlety.

She moves along the CD racks, pauses at every sixth disc and removes it. Only when there are enough gaps, does she randomly replace them.

Nothing much is out of place, but it is enough of a taste of chaos, she's sure, to deeply upset Leo and force him to see that living with her cannot work.

On the stroke of six, Leo arrives and presents her with a large bunch of cream roses, the same type she carried in her bridal bouquet. Deborah admires them briefly and then places them on the drainer, intending to dump them in the bin when Leo is not looking.

'And what home improvements have we made today, my darling?'

His joviality raises her hackles.

'You know how to put a stop to this, Leo.'

'Maybe I don't want to. Maybe you're going to have to accept the fact that I'm in love with you. That I want to spend the rest of my life with you.'

Deborah offers Leo a sickly smile. 'I'm afraid I finished the gin last night.'

'In that case, I'll go and listen to some music.'

Again, Deborah waits for the explosion of anger, the final argument that will drive her husband out. Nothing. She sits on the bottom stair, opposite the dining room door and listens to *Tristan and Isolde*, remembering the night Leo took her to see it. As the curtain fell, she wept at the cruelty of it all.

When the opera is over, Leo appears and takes her hands in his. 'Why don't you forget this silliness, Deb, and come to bed with me?'

'You're not bothered about your CDs?'

'Hardly.'

Deborah grimaces with frustration. 'What do I

have to do, Leo?'

He gently squeezes her fingers between his.

'You could stop this silly war and be my wife again.'

Something bursts inside Deborah. She can't go on like this. Can't go forward or back. She lets herself be led upstairs, where Leo undresses her and lays her down on the bed. Once more, Deborah tenses under Leo's touch. She climbs into the secret portion of herself that is her own domain and lets her husband go to work on her numb body. He tries his best to please, until she pushes him away because she is sore and tired and wishing she'd never given in.

In the early hours of the morning, with the moonlight easing through the curtains and smoothing out the faults that time has written into their bodies, Leo draws her into a tight embrace.

'I told you I could make everything all right, didn't I?'

Deborah lies still, like she used to in the old days. She remains separate from her body, her old means to an end.

'You know, one day, we'll look back on this and laugh. The campaign you waged to try and force me out of my own... our own house.' Leo laces his fingers through Deborah's and sighs with satisfaction.

And that's when she sees what she's been missing all along. The real victory, beneath her nose all the time.

She leans into him and whispers softly into his ear. In the half-light, confession doesn't feel so bad. And she has no expectation of absolution, so she's doubly free.

When Deborah is finished explaining her past on the estate and the things she did to survive, she turns to Leo and waits. He probably believes the dawn shadows hide his moment of doubt, the sudden shift of his facial gears as he leans over to cover her forehead and eyes in kisses. He pauses for a second at her mouth and then presses his lips to hers, parting them with his tongue.

His breath isn't full of her, as she expects. Deborah tastes instead the sweet, rank tang of souring milk. She turns away, smiling, grateful that she's laid the foundations for her divorce at last.

Voices

Tommy's voice deepens early. His hips jut out, forcing him into the lumbering gait of the newborn calf. Along with these changes, a lava flow rises. Tommy only knows that anger is a currency, that threat has value. His classmates point behind his back, laughing, but worried. He is 'the naughty boy', both mocked and feared.

The lava flow has voices. Voices that cajole. Voices that accuse and command. Voices that cannot be ignored, however much he tries.

He leaves his chair, crossing the classroom to drop down next to Donald, the new boy. Donald shrinks back, already aware of Tommy's reputation.

Tommy puts his ear against the other boy's skull. He listens. Nothing. Just the swell and roar of his own head. Donald holds his breath until his cheeks and lips turn lilac.

Their teacher darts forward, slicing the air with her squeal. Tommy obeys dumbly, returning to his table. His less-than-splendid isolation.

One day, Donald and some of the other boys dare Tommy to look up Teacher's skirt. He waits until she is sat at her desk and then rolls his pencil so that it comes to rest between her court shoes.

Tommy, what are you doing?

Just fetching my pencil, Miss.

He looks up, but her legs are crossed. His memory grabs at little details – the lace-trimmed legs of her knickers squashed against the sheen of her honey-coloured tights.

Miss, Tommy's... A chorus of external voices rise against him.

Miss, Tommy's got his head under your desk! Miss, he's looking up your skirt!

Miss yells until the headmaster comes running. With his raging, sobbing denials Tommy gives more entertainment than his classmates ever hoped for. As he is dragged away by his ear, the class cheer and whistle.

He is sent home for the rest of the week. Mother comes to collect him. She locks him in his room without anything to eat, until he promises to go to confession. Even then, she constantly rants at him, telling him he is dirty and evil. That, if he wasn't too strong for her, she'd give him a bath with carbolic soap and the floor scrubber, until all his dirtiness is washed away.

At Church, Tommy enters the dim box and slides back the shutter to begin his confession.

I have been angry. I have had lustful thoughts. I have played with myself. The other boys dared me to look up the teacher's skirt, Father.

Father, I hear voices. In the night. Father, I cannot sleep.

Instead of the usual lecture on the evils of lust and self-pollution, the priest relays to Tommy the story of Joan of Arc, who heard voices from heaven. How they guided her, so that she led the French Dauphin to victory over the scurrilous English.

Tommy makes an act of contrition, once again promising faithfully to keep his hands above the bed covers.

Outside, in the nave of the church, the voices resume.

Tommy falls to the tiles, cheek flattened against their cool, like some mystic overcome by the fever of God's love.

At home, a doctor appears, with white hands and icy metal instruments. Tommy still burns, floating in and out of delirium. The lava boils beneath his skin.

An eruption approaches.

He hears unfamiliar words, part of the code that adults share. A code he cannot crack.

Ado-les-sense. Pu-ber-tee.

In rare silence, Tommy dreams of Joan in her masculine armour, dreams of the soft-cheeked Dauphin, led to power by the hand of a shepherd-ess. He wakes, shrieking. Escaping the flames. Avoiding burning with Joan at the scurrilous English stake.

His fever breaks. Mother forces him out of bed, orders him downstairs in his scratchy pyjamas.

Upright at the kitchen table, Tommy's head blooms with voices once again. Mother compounds them by giving him yet another lecture about impurity. He tries to listen to her voice, rather than to any of the others infecting his head. But they're too strong for him. They drown out her weak signal and he loses her frequency.

Tommy jams the heels of his hands into his eyes, trying to ignore the carving knife glittering on the scrubbed pine table. Mother turns her back on him, rolling out pastry for tonight's pie. She twitters about a boy's duties, about how he should protect and cherish her, rather than bring shame and trouble to her doorstep. How he's not the son she asked for in her prayers.

Tommy grabs the knife.

It needs a home. A sheath. Leaving it lying around is asking for trouble.

Mother's skin melts like butter.

It isn't much. A stripe of crimson blood across her neck. Tommy drops the knife as she screams. He stops his ears with his hands.

Always screaming. Shush Mother. Don't cry. My head screams for the both of us.

But she does not stop until help comes.

They will lock him up. They march him from the house with his arms pulled tight across his back. The neighbours gather to watch the show, heads bowing with disapproval.

The faint scar on his mother's neck is a badge of shame. It is not the wounding that she holds against him. It is the stigma. Her son. The madman.

In the cool of the van, the vacancy of the huge, square ambulance, the voices whisper softly, congratulating him, praising his skill, promising reward. From nowhere, crystal tears roll down his cheeks. His arms throb in their restraints.

Tommy has never seen the country before. Now he glimpses it in slivers, as the van judders along the gravel drive, coming to a stop before the Victorian institute they have assigned him to.

One of the ambulance men asks him if he understands what he has done, where he is now and why. Tommy sinks to his knees, begins his Confiteor, weeping all the while. The ambulance men shake their heads and drag him inside. A heavy lock turns behind him.

He expects it to be hell, but it is paradise. Behind closed doors, he and his voices solemnly commune. His mother is already a ghost, a memory of a half-remembered life.

Starched angels glide down endless blank corridors. They speak firmly and fairly, with cool professional compassion. A doctor attends him, producing from his pocket a sharp needle, a full syringe.

Silence presses like cotton wool to his mouth, his nose, his eyes, his ears. Tommy gulps for breath and then sinks back into sleep.

There are no voices.

When he wakes, it is to silence. Without rage, without the fire behind his eyeballs. An angel tells him his mother is here. They lead him down to a bare room – a table, two chairs, a bulky orderly in the corner.

His mother wears a navy hat; its sharp angles

are softened by netting. She speaks in a low voice, in halting phrases that drift across the table to him, extinguished before they reach his ears.

Tommy's head is now made of iron. Gravity pulls it to the floor. He struggles to remember what the angel told him.

Smile. Be nice. Answer her questions.

It has taken her an hour to get here. The expense has been considerable. She mouths the words to no effect.

He tries to focus on his mother's face, to ignore the angry scar on her neck. But the scar is simple, complete. Easy to contemplate. While her eyes and mouth chase each other across her face in an endless cat-and-mouse.

Laughter is his only response. Soon laughter becomes convulsions, becomes tears and screams.

She doesn't make the effort to visit again.

The medication stops working. Once more, the voices howl and rage. They strap Tommy down and pierce his brain with electricity. His temples crisp like chicken skin.

He crawls back to his bed. The world becomes permanent night. He is thrown down. Weak. Useless. Ghostly. He longs for the flame of ado-les-sense, the power of pu-ber-tee. Alone in the darkness, he longs for his voices, to supply the things he needs to say. His tongue is knotted like a rope.

There are three meals a day. A nurse to help him shave, to wash. Simple work, when he is well enough. Rest when he is not.

The voices of the damned are dampened by soundproofing.

They tell him he is a man now. Angels and doctors smile on him, offering encouragement.

They tell Tommy the voices have left him alone for many years. There is talk of going home. The angels help him write a letter as if he is back at school, doing composition exercises.

If it is posted, Tommy does not know. He is never made aware of a reply. The subject of home is dropped. Instead, he is offered work. Outside. A chance to live in the real world again, eight hours a day.

Tommy's hand trembles, as he is led to the front door, as the huge brass latch is lifted, as daylight and the smell of freshly mown grass leak in. The sunlight tastes of hope, the grass smells of freedom. There is a white bus to take him and others to the world.

He waves discreetly at the redbrick hospital as it recedes out of view. He fancies that it blinks a tear from one of its shuttered eyes.

Filing is a woman's job. Tommy hasn't obedient fingers or the sense of order needed to make a success of it. He would be better out in the workshop, at the lathe. But his medical notes dictate otherwise.

So, he remains in the air-conditioned cool of the office, among the weeping cheese plants, the ringing phones and typewriters.

He throws down a set of files, angry at their

rebellion. Tommy is always obedient, always good. First to his voices, who he thinks have deserted him, and now to the doctors, to the angels of the hospital. And to this sparse-haired, thickly moustached man, in his shiny, shiny suit and wrinkled shoes. It is unfair that the files won't co-operate, that he has to count on his fingers as he recites the alphabet in his head, before one carbon sheet can find a home. By the end of the day, he has only cleared a third of his pile.

Never mind, says the secretary, all blonde hair and red lips. They'll still be there tomorrow.

He recalls the secretary as he lies in bed. He shapes her from air, gives her weight with his heightened senses. She's next to him, sharing his blanket. An alien shape, delineated by bra, slip and stockings. He and the secretary press their faces together, open and close their lips in a mysterious rhythm. She takes his hand and guides it under her slip, where she keeps a secret world.

A new sensation breaks through the medicated fug.

This is what he has been missing. Another body, different to his.

Her smiles linger. She touches Tommy at every available opportunity. At first, he is afraid. At first, her hand feels like an insect crawling across his flesh. He feels the old lava rise, the whisper of a voice. He shakes this down.

She helps him with the filing, showing him how to organise things more quickly. They eat lunch together, knees brushing against each other almost casually.

One night, as the men clock off, the secretary takes hold of Tommy's hand. She asks him to stay, though he has ten minutes until his bus leaves. Heat crackles across Tommy's skin and he sees himself reflected in her eyes.

He agrees to stay.

The secretary offers to lock up, leaving the boss man free to visit his mistress. After the last person is gone, she draws down the office blind and locks them inside.

There is no prelude, no small talk. She hitches up her skirt and he drops to his knees, begins a feral groping. When she is tired of this, she beckons for him to stand, pushes him back onto the desk, unbuttons his trousers and mounts him.

It is over in minutes. The secretary disentangles herself, straightens her clothing and lights a cigarette. Tommy moves in to kiss her, but she turns her head to one side. Her eyes are blank, where minutes ago he saw himself.

He wants to offer her something. To reconnect. What is it women want? Flowers? Rings? Dinner?

Dinner?

The secretary looks at Tommy, considers his offer for a moment and then laughs once, from the back of her throat, dry and hoarse.

We could...

He does not continue. She is utterly disinterested, flicking flakes of ash from her skirt. Running a hand through her hair.

Picking up his coat, Tommy snatches at the door handle. He looks pleadingly at her, but she forces him to wait while she finishes her smoke. Then, with a shrug of her shoulders, she unlocks the door.

Rain glosses the city streets, as Tommy stomps through puddles, soaking the turn-ups on his trousers. In the pocket of his hand-me-down jacket is a note, telling him what to do in an emergency. The letters bleed into each other, robbing him of his escape route.

Tommy is lost. Freedom does not figure in his desires.

His crotch feels sticky, dirty. He walks awkwardly, burning with the knowledge of another human being.

There will be trouble back home. He is certain of that. They will cast him out, when all Tommy wants is to be locked back up, to be reinstalled in that silent, simple space.

Better to stay away than to invite more trouble.

On his way to nowhere, he passes a smart row of Georgian town houses, their stone steps glistening with rain and sodium light. Open curtains offer him a glimpse of a future he's excluded from. A family sitting together, watching TV, in a bright yellow room, on huge, marshmallowy sofas. Before he can think about it, before he knows quite what he is doing, he unlatches the gate, climbs the stairs and presses his face to the rain-streaked glass.

There is no desire to frighten or confuse. To

menace. Tommy simply drinks in the moment. Observes everything he is not.

The rain chills his bones.

The family don't look up. Why would they? Everything they need is in their room.

Their voices, their laughter are silenced by the thick glass. The world outside is nothing but a phantom. Only their safe space is real.

Crushed, he moves on.

Under the railway arches, Tommy finds a brazier. Grateful for a snatch of warmth, he pauses, holds his hands over the flames.

Here people inhabit the shadows, amid sodden blankets and cardboard.

A gruff voice and dirt-engrained hands offer him a swig of cider. An image of himself, twenty years from now.

He hesitates, remembering alcohol and medication don't mix. But medication and the outside world don't mix either.

The cider has its own sweet way of making him forget.

The Naming of Gods

The Germans arrived on Sunday morning, sweeping through the hall and into the dorms with their backpacks and bedrolls. Their English hosts looked on, overwhelmed by their noise, their exoticism, their bright clothes, hard consonants and ugly footwear.

Andreas entered the hall with silent dignity. Tall and broad-shouldered, his jaw was strong and his hair white-blond. Sapphire light sparkled in his eyes.

'Hello,' said James, offering his hand, 'I'll show you to the dorm.'

Andreas smiled uncertainly and held out his overfull holdall. Bob, the exchange organiser, intervened.

'Thanks James, but Andreas is one of our leaders. He's with the rest of us. This way, Andreas.'

Andreas. Andreas. Andreas. James pronounced it slowly, drawing out the last syllable, unwilling to let go of it. In the theology books that he read for fun, names were magical. They gave you power over their owners.

The fortnight-long exchange began with the usual sort of icebreakers. In the Parachute Game, as the red and blue silk tented upwards, James threw himself under the canopy, bumping into as many bodies as he could. He always ensured he pitched up next to Andreas, deliberately flouting the game's intention. After all, he had already made his most important introduction. He didn't need to get to know anyone else.

At dinner, the English boys and girls reserved James a seat. He shrugged them off, finding to his delight a space next to his new friend. He took extra portions of salami and devoured it enthusiastically, gratified by Andreas's nods of approval.

When the other leaders sloped off to bed, Andreas appeared in the hall with his guitar. The German and English boys groaned and made themselves scarce, leaving James and the girls to form a circle around Andreas.

They sang everything from *Hey Jude* to James's favourite, *California Dreaming*. When Andreas harmonised in his bright, clear tenor, James melted and pooled across the parquet. Reading the rapt faces of the English girls, he foresaw a battle for the German's affections.

Day two began with defeat. Lisa, a loud, brash girl with ringlets and freckles, usurped James's place at Andreas's right hand. James contemplated the cruellest ways in which he could silence her shrieking giggles. He pushed away his toast untouched. Disappointment knotted up his stomach.

After breakfast, the dorms had to be tidied before their first excursion. A shopping centre hardly seemed a cultural highlight, even if it was the largest in Europe. Yet the Germans filed out to their mini-buses enthusiastically, bursting into song as they swung out of the drive. James's heavy heart portended disaster. During the journey, he re-ingratiated himself with the English, afraid of having to trail round the shops alone.

The girls loved James. They wanted him to be their brother and told him their boyfriend woes. Together, they shopped for clothes, asking James's advice, letting him pick their lingerie. They kissed him on the cheek and walked arm-in-arm with him, saying how nice it was to know a boy 'they could talk to.' James smiled politely, all the while repeating his mantra under his breath. Andreas, Andreas, Andreas...

Watching in shop windows, James shivered at any blond reflection that passed, hoping his magic would take effect.

They lunched on burgers. This was bad enough, but the noise from the indoor funfair was unbearable. James sighed. If Andreas was here, he felt sure he could suffer anything. Why was life so unfair?

'You okay, Jimmy? You look a bit pale.'

James jolted back into the moment, his eyes narrowing with displeasure at Lisa's faux concern.

'I didn't sleep much.'

'Me neither. I was talking to Andreas. He's gorgeous, isn't he?'

'Is he?'

'Well, I think he is. I'm going to get off with him.'

'No chance.'

'What?'

'Well he's older, isn't he?' James struggled to keep the wobble from his voice.

Lisa wound a strand of hair round her finger and popped the end of it in her mouth, 'Only four years. Nothing much.'

'Still...'

Lisa yawned. 'Do you want to go back to the bus for a nap?'

He refused. How could he share space with his competition? Rising to his feet, James collected up the debris of their meal. As he placed the emptied tray on the counter-top, he became aware of a presence behind him. *His* presence. James swung round to find Andreas standing over him, the soft down on his forearms iridescent under the strip lighting.

'You are very... oh... um...' Andreas paused, groping for his word.

Say beautiful, willed James. Say gorgeous. Say, 'You are very the first love of me.' James adored the uncertain syntax of German English. Genders seemed to mean nothing to them.

'...Responsible.' Andreas beamed. James, however, heard the ping as the dullest adjective in the world bounced off his brittle heart.

Day three followed a night of anxious waiting. Andreas had been worryingly absent. Added to this, the forty young people were about to split into groups, travelling to various locations. If James and Andreas were in different groups...

Bob posted the lists in the main hall before breakfast. Everyone crowded around them, James at the back, his tongue stuck to the roof of his mouth, his palms slick with sweat.

It was as he feared. Bollocks! He was allocated to group A, Andreas to group C along with Lisa and Caroline who last night declared themselves the founding members of the Andreas Fan Club. In frustration, James kicked the wall and then winced at the pain in his foot.

Still silently repeating Andreas's name, James took a pen from his pocket, calmly crossed out Caroline's name and wrote his own in its place.

He reached the minibus minutes before departure. Would the only seat left be up front, next to Andreas? Only this prize would improve the excursion. Maybe they would have to share a tent, pitching it together, sleeping bags side-by-side, mouths inches apart...

What the fuck?

There was Caroline, vacuous cow, fawning over James's German, flicking her hair over her shoulders with one hand, while brushing Andreas's golden arm with the other. James dropped his bag on the tarmac and yanked open the minibus door.

'Out.'

'What?'

'You have to get out, Caroline.'

This dampened her laughter. James caught Lisa's sour, intrigued expression in the seat behind.

'What is this?' Andreas looked cuter than ever with his forehead furrowed in confusion. He rubbed his jaw.

James felt his cheeks colour. 'Bob says that Caroline has to go with group A. Too many girls in this group, apparently.'

He thought he saw a flicker of recognition in Andreas's eyes. The German reached over the defeated Caroline and unclicked her seatbelt. 'We must do as Bob says, Fraulein Caroline.'

Caroline opened her mouth to protest, but Andreas silenced her with a look.

'We must be motoring.'

James placed his bag on the warm seat as Caroline elbowed past him with wet eyes. He grinned with triumph. Andreas smiled also, but did not help him fasten his belt.

The Lake District was a washout. Torrential rain and a thick mist, which clung jealously to the mountains. And Andreas had his own one-man tent, which meant that James had to top and tail with Colin, who had bad breath and stinking feet. It was a relief to escape at six in the morning, darting across the sodden, shit-spattered field to the showers. Standing for an age under the hot dribble of water, thinking of Andreas. Rinsing away the soap from his body, the fetid atmosphere of his miserable tent.

They spent two days listening to a rainy timpani on the minibus roof, viewing the towns of the Lake District from waterlogged car parks. Even Lisa's loud enthusiasm shrank away.

'The English weather,' muttered the other Germans. Andreas smiled softly, leaving the van intermittently to, inexplicably, brave the rain. Parting was agony. James settled back into his seat and dreamed of Andreas, miserable on some lonely slope. It was hell without him. Sometimes, James believed he would rise, throw open the minibus door and go after his blonde German but, at the moment of commitment, his nerve failed him.

As they left Keswick behind them, the damp travellers were glad to see the sun emerge. By the time they reached their next destination – a stone-built cottage nestling in the Cheviots – their spirits were revived.

Dinner had to be prepared and James volunteered himself, attempting to peel potatoes by Andreas's side.

Practical matters had always eluded him. Sure enough, his arms went limp, his fingers turned to tubes of jelly. Wet potatoes slipped from his hand. And when he managed to hold on, James dug the peeler deeper into the vegetable than he intended.

'Useless.'

'What?'

'I can't do it.'

'Huh?'

James patiently explained that he was a books and ideas boy.

'Books? *Langweilig.*' The German put his hand to his mouth and yawned exaggeratedly. 'We must do.'

With that, Andreas reached round James, placing a hand over his. 'Hold like this, ja?'

'Yes.'

'Now, like this.' With his left hand, Andreas guided the peeler so that, under their combined effort, the potato skin shrugged away from the waxy flesh underneath.

'Now, James.'

James shook his head. 'I think I need to see again.'

Andreas sighed. 'OK.'

Lisa clattered in. 'What you two up to?'

It sounded so much like an accusation that they broke apart, peeler and potato bouncing on the tiled floor.

'I was helping James with her kartoffel... uhm, po...'

'...tato,' offered James, cheated again.

'Can't you do it? Here, it's easy.' With this, Lisa pushed James to one side and began peeling.

'I'll just go then, shall I?'

James could not bear their laughter. He sought sanctuary in the garden, returning reluctantly for dinner. Lisa once more looked triumphant at Andreas's side. James toyed with his food and then announced he was having an early night. His patience had worn thin and his desire to slap her ugly face itched on his palm.

Next day, the Roman fort was extremely dull. This was not the kind of ancient history that interested James. This was definitely *langweilig*. There was so little of it left. Just a couple of inches of random rubble. And his imagination was not in an obliging mood.

The Germans seemed impressed. They clambered over former guardrooms and bathhouses, shouting what sounded like rude comments to each other. Such an odd, cumbersome language, James thought. Everyone seemed to be enjoying themselves, while James remained apart and embarrassed.

Andreas and Lisa were nowhere to be seen. So, James stomped back to the minibus and contemplated the situation.

His mantra had failed him. So much for Eastern wisdom! What he needed was some good old god-of-vengeance slaughter and retribution to assuage his pain.

At lunchtime, everyone returned and James had to give up his silence. Lisa and Andreas arrived last, red-faced and breathless.

'Lisa has been showing me the country of you. He's very, very extreme in his beauty.'

James squashed the impulse to correct Andreas. His stomach lurched at the proffered plate of smoked meat, the same lunch they had eaten for the past week. It seemed the visitors' desire for their own cuisine was unquenchable.

James took the plate and sighed. To his surprise, Andreas did not leave his side, but placed his own plate on his knees and began to eat, tearing at the bread with his fine white teeth.

'You like Lisa then, Andreas?'

'Oh yes. He is a very lovely girl.' James's heart

sank. He was about to say, 'You mean *she*,' when Andreas spoke again.

'But...' Andreas paused, looked about him, and then looked directly into James's eyes.

'Yes?'

'Sometimes, he is noisy. He does not know quiet, like you.'

'She is noisy. But she likes you. She told me.'

'Hm...'

James could not bear to misinterpret the sad look on Andreas's face, the way he stopped chewing and his jaw slackened.

'What's the matter?'

'We return to our homes already.'

'You mean soon?'

'Ja!' They laughed, and Andreas turned away.

Thinking their conference over, James bit into a tomato. Juice and seeds squirted over his chin. Andreas pulled a hanky from his pocket and dabbed at the mess, causing James to flush. His knees slipped away from him. He was grateful he was sitting down.

'You and me,' Andreas said, folding away the hanky, 'walk together after the meal. I think we may be good friends.'

'Do you? Yes. Yes let's.' James put down his plate. 'Let's go now.' Food seemed unnecessary, especially muck like this.

That was the first of many walks. They ambled as close together as James could bear, without touching. Returning to base, James revelled in his victory over the Andreas fan club. He would never have risked openly applying for membership, yet his bloodless coup had left him president.

The days flashed past. Activities such as shopping and rock-climbing, singing and orienteering were all just stepping-stones to their next encounter.

James patiently helped with Andreas's English, while Andreas taught him filthy German words. In order to get their meaning across, Andreas mimed, causing James to blush and shriek with laughter. For *blasen*, Andreas moved his fist rapidly back and forth, inches from his mouth, tongue bulging in his cheek. At first James did not get it. Andreas pointed to his crotch and then repeated the gesture.

'Oh. Yes. Of course.' James's cheeks glowed. He let out a low whistle, a release of excitement and agony.

James rarely spoke to any of the English gang. Every so often, he caught Lisa glaring at him, Caroline's arm slung round her shoulders. He sat next to Andreas in the evenings, turning the songbook pages for him. One sight of the girls and James would beam and wave, ecstatic to see them enraged.

On the last night of the exchange there was a Christian service, with songs from the musical *Godspell*. Pitta bread and red grape juice were distributed amongst the teenagers, in an atmosphere of deep melancholy. In two weeks they had all forged intense bonds, the typically accelerated friendships of late adolescence. Girls and boys huddled together, holding hands. Tears flowed freely. Hugs and kisses were exchanged.

Andreas sat on the floor next to James. Moved by the horror of parting, James inched closer, so that their knees touched. Andreas smiled and closed his eyes, apparently praying.

When he was sure that Lisa was watching, James laid his head on Andreas's shoulder. From this privileged position he could hear the rhythm of Andreas's breathing, inhale his aftershave. If the rest of the group noticed and wondered, James did not care. For these few hours at least, he would have his man.

The night ended all too quickly, and the leaders, including Andreas, were strict in enforcing bedtime. Everyone was travelling tomorrow and needed their sleep. James tucked himself into his sleeping bag reluctantly, wondering when Andreas would make his move.

Breakfast was punctuated by more sobs and hugs. James watched with detachment, knowing that these professions of love and friendship were nothing. He had the real thing.

Andreas caught his eye and smiled.

As he washed his breakfast dishes, James once more became aware of Andreas, standing behind him. He waited for the German to speak, aware of Andreas's hot breath prickling on his neck.

'Come mit me.'

This lapse indicated that Andreas was agitated. James followed, hardly daring to breathe, in case he scared Andreas at the crucial moment.

The general commotion of leaving meant that no one saw them slip away.

'Where are we going, Andreas?'

'Ssh. The he's and she's must not notice.'

At last, at last, it was their time. They could make this work. What challenge was the North Sea when you had love?

James galloped down the stairs, matching Andreas's pace.

They headed to the bathroom, Andreas dropping the door latch behind them.

'Sit. I have something to show you.' Andreas patted the seat next to him. James complied. Andreas sighed, while James struggled to stay silent. He was aware of his body and outside of it at the same time. All he could focus on was Andreas's mouth, his pale lips and perfect teeth.

'Andreas, I...'

'Ssh, James. This is very heavy for me. You know I like you and you know how much.'

'Yes, yes, I do.'

Andreas stretched an arm round James's quivering shoulders, causing him to twitch with desire. He didn't know how long he could hold back the tidal wave.

'Gut. I want to share with you.'

Andreas leaned forward, his face inches from James. The boy closed his eyes and tilted his head back, listening to his heart thunder in his ears. Other parts of him stirred.

Andreas took his left hand and closed James's fingers over his palm. 'Look.'

In his hand was a small photograph. James turned it over. An elfin Germanic face stared up at him. Ice blue eyes and dyed blonde hair, severely cropped. The resemblance was remarkable.

'Sister?' James's voice shrunk to a pale squeak. '*Schwester?*'

'No.' Andreas shook his head, beaming broadly. '*Freundin.*'

Girlfriend.

The photo became like molten lead in his hand.

'I'm sorry, Andreas. Entschuldigung... bitte.'

James struggled to his feet, without looking back. With each step across the hall, he attempted to erase his memory. Andreas's lean body, the smell of his skin, the security that his arm provided. None of it was any use now.

James had to pack and there was his share of the cleaning up to do. He would work hard. Do his duty.

And he would not cry.

Lisa was waiting for him in the English minibus.

'You okay Jimmy?'

He forced himself to smile and nodded. 'You never got to snog Andreas, did you?'

Lisa frowned and shrugged, leaning into James's ear, whispering, 'To be honest, I think he might be a bit... well... gay!'

James turned to the window and blinked away tears before she had chance to notice.

The Gift

Ten to eight on Christmas Eve and I'm cradling a glass of single malt. As usual, I've bought the biggest tree I can drag through my door. Its baubles sparkle and glow in firelight and my parcels look suitably inviting stacked around its base.

Childhood Christmases haunt me like banshees. The phone stays off the hook. At this blessed time, my ghosts have a habit of materialising in distinctly fleshy form. They're usually bought off with a twenty-pound note and a litre bottle of vodka, but why take the risk?

So now it's Me-Mass. A feast for one.

Nat King Cole wishes me a merry little Christmas in velvet tones. I'm floating in a Me-Mass bubble of soft focus contentment. Tomorrow is a day for lounging in front of the TV with a huge box of Thornton's chocs and a bottle of Bollinger. In the evening, I'll crack open my Fortnum hamper and catch the last repeat of the Queen's Speech, offering Old Liz a horizontal salute.

My bubble bursts with a knock on the door. A debt collector's thud. The walls, and my chest, shudder.

Gathering my wits in my whisky glass, I rise only to nudge the volume up. The door sounds again. And again. Louder and louder, until the vibration rings in my ears.

Oh, for God's sake, just go away!

Only Mother could be this persistent, but the last I heard, she was squatting under a railway arch in the Midlands. That was a few years ago and her liver was almost pâté then, so I'm fairly sure she's not standing on the other side of my panelled door.

The last time she appeared, she howled like a dog until I let her in. This was in another town, another delicious suburb. My 'for sale' sign soon went up after she was caught rifling through my neighbour's rubbish and having a crap in their Koi pond.

I didn't leave a forwarding address, but she has a homing instinct that would put most pigeons to shame. Several new addresses later, I'm convinced that she's done it again.

The knock comes once more, shrinking my resistance.

I drag myself up from the sofa and mooch down the hall. Then I peer through the spyglass into the shadows cast by my porch-light.

A creamy eyeball meets mine. My heart hammers against my ribs.

On the other side of the door, Mother sighs. Except I've never heard this one before. Mother has a soft sigh which indicates what a hard life she's had. She has a judgemental sigh when her son lets her down yet again. But my personal favourite is the sigh that heralds her descent into unconsciousness.

This is none of the above. This sigh is that of the weary, the genuinely in pain. It finds an echo in me and I'm stabbed with curiosity.

'Mother?' I have to be certain this isn't one of her ruses.

There's a moment of excruciating silence, a rustle and fumbling.

'I'm sorry to bother you, Sir...'

Mother has called me many things in her time, but never 'sir' – not even in her mostly alcoholically unctuous moments.

'Are you still there, Sir? I hope you are! You see, I have a gift for you.'

A gift? For me? What – a diamond as big as my fist? A Caribbean cruise for two with the companion of my choice? The news that Mother has finally made it to the great pub in the sky, where the drinks are free and last orders is never called?

The door is a fortress of locks and bolts. I slide back the first of them. Perhaps my past troubles are being rewarded. Perhaps tonight's the night when Me-Mass becomes Christmas again.

Perhaps I've just drunk far too much whisky.

'Could you leave my gift on the step for me? I don't usually open the door after 8pm. You can't be too careful these days.'

'Oh indeed, Sir. We live in troubled times. But I'm afraid Sir, it's the sort of gift I have to give you personally.'

'Really?'

'Please, Sir, open up. I'm so wanting to share this gift with you.'

I wince at the Americanism, but it's a relief. This can't be one of Mother's ruses. She is the most eloquent drunk you could ever meet, holding forth on the state of the world in the clipped tones of a wartime BBC broadcaster. Never a slip of grammar between glass and lip.

'Just a minute.' I slide back bolts and chains, turn various keys, my cynicism softened. Through the spy-hole, I watch the woman step forward in anticipation.

Shadows do her no favours. They don't soften the angles of her face, or her hatchet-parted hair. She is middle-aged and her protruding eyes and down-turned mouth communicate profound sorrow. Such a contrast to the false brightness of her voice.

I know I should shut the door again. Nothing good can come of this.

'Ah, Sir, it's so good to see you face-to-face.' She offers me a frozen hand, which I shake quickly, looking around for my reward. All I can see is a large leather folio, tucked beneath her arm.

'Good evening. I'm Noreen and I'm here to-night to deliver to you the most important gift you'll ever receive.'

Oh goody, here it comes. I almost close my eyes and hold out my hands, like a kid.

'I want to give you your copy of our leaflet.'

This is it?

Wow.

The magic of Christmas strikes again.

'Thanks, Noreen, but I've got leaflets coming out of my ears. Pizza parlours, Chinese take-aways, a guaranteed second income of £250 to £1,000 a week. Piles of glossy-coated information stream through my letter box, seven days a week, fifty-two weeks a year.' I pause and sigh, in an attempt to echo my caller's desperation. 'Some-times, I want to take a roll of gaffer tape and seal the letter box up. To stop the paper terrorism. Oh, won't somebody stop the paper terrorism!'

She's not moving. Her face is all bovine sub-mission. We stand for a moment contemplating each other. I smile at her in a sickly, patronising way. Then I go to shut the door, but eyes continue to plead with me. Perhaps I haven't made myself clear enough. Perhaps I'm not as tough as I thought.

'You're not the first to react in this way, Sir. But, if you could just open your mind...'

'What about your family? It's Christmas Eve. What sort of a night is it to be delivering leaflets?'

The woman drops her head and retracts her tract.

Even I, in my glowing, Me-Mass haze, can see I've upset her. An icy blast curls round us both. Noreen's sallow cheeks are stung with the cold.

'You must excuse me, sometimes, I get a lit-tle...' I grope for the word, but it's beyond my reach. My thoughts are lazy, my diction flabby.

I'm perched on the rim of drunkenness and I want to dive in.

Noreen shakes her head. 'Angry?'

Her diagnosis slaps me soberly in the face.

'Yes, I suppose...'

'That's why you need this leaflet, Sir.' She reaches out again.

'I suppose it'll change my life.'

'That's the idea.' Her voice is strangely hollow, her evangelistic zeal congealed.

Noreen puts the thing into my hand. I pull away and turn it to the light. There's a smiling Jesus, embracing people of all hues. A child-like rainbow straddles them, each colour represented by a broad bold stripe. Everyone is wearing a sickly grin. I read the title aloud.

'Armageddon is coming: are you ready?'

Behind the love-fest float images of starvation, murder and nuclear annihilation.

'Wow. Now that's one hardcore leaflet.'

My new lady friend shoots me a look of disapproval. The hall grows quiet as my CD gives way to silence. Somewhere in this dark night, my mother is warming herself by a makeshift brazier, or sleeping in a cardboard box, with only a bottle of Polish vodka for comfort. Or she's stiff by a canal bank, awaiting a rabid dog, or an illicitly courting couple to discover her.

Mrs Evangelist gathers herself up and opens her mouth, about to put her Jesus hard sell on me. But I know all about him. My mother raised me as a Catholic – a fact that infuriated my dad so much he left not long after my baptism.

'Listen, it's too cold to be debating this on the doorstep. Why don't you come inside and have a drink?'

'No, that's fine, Sir. My willingness to suffer for Jesus is part of my testimony.'

'And my Jesus wouldn't want you to suffer.' I reach for her hand and draw her in, ignoring the look of alarm on her face.

The leaflet slips from my hands and falls onto the tiles. When I look down, I see that Jesus's face bears the imprint of his disciple's thick-soled boot.

'Come and have a drink. We'll celebrate your boss's birthday.'

'I don't drink. It is against the rules...'

'Splendid.'

It's just the provocation I need.

I never touch booze during the long, monotonous months of everyday life. But, come high days and holy days, I descend into a cavern of inebriation. I'm not like my mother. I don't dedicate the whole of my life to it. Just those times when I'm supposed to be happy.

'So, what'll it be Noreen? Scotch, Gin or Champagne?'

Touched by her concern for my immortal soul, I want to reciprocate with my own brand of generosity. Although she's not getting my Bollinger. Supermarket champagne only for the evangelist.

Noreen places her folio down on the rug, by her feet. Her arms hug her body but her eyes vault around the room. Despite herself, she looks impressed.

'I'm sorry about your leaflet.'

She gives a hollow little laugh and taps her folio with the toe of her boot. 'Don't be. There's a hundred more in there. And boxes and boxes of them back at Church. A roomful.'

Noreen's zeal has completely vaporised.

'Have a drink with me?'

She raises her hand. 'I really don't...'

'I'm not taking no for an answer. Jesus always drank wine.'

She smiles and her face softens under the fire-light.

'This room is really nicely done.'

I hand her a glass of champers. No one's ever complemented my Christmas decorations before. Mother always just pulled a face and sank another drink.

'D'you know, Mr...?'

'Call me Ed.'

'D'you know, Ed, I've not drunk since I joined the church. And that was ten years ago.'

'Ten years is a long time.'

'Not long enough, for some.' Noreen looks down at her boots and cradles her glass but doesn't raise it to her mouth.

I get to my feet, holding up my champagne for a toast. 'To Jesus. Happy birthday to him. Happy birthday to him. Happy birthday, dear Jesus...'

Noreen gives me a long, frozen stare and then touches the glass to her lips, grimacing as she does so. Here we are, two strangers thrown together on Christmas Eve. Despite my Me-Mass bubble having burst, I like it. It feels...ordained.

'I'm sorry if I scared you out there. I'm not used to visitors.'

Noreen nods. 'Well, thank you, Ed. It's nice to be warm.'

I shrug. 'No bother. Why wait for Armageddon to receive your reward?'

She smiles awkwardly. I'm hit by the sort of lightning-bolt of perception that only a skin-full of alcohol can produce.

'You're not entirely happy, are you Noreen?'

Her eyes fill with tears as she lifts them to the ceiling, suddenly captivated by my intricate ceiling-rose.

'It's fine...' she shrugs. Here comes that heart-squeezing sigh again. 'Only... I hate this time of year.'

'Me too.'

'All those happy family images. Gathered round a Christmas tree to open presents, stuffing themselves full of turkey. It makes me feel like a... freak.'

'Snap!'

'What about your family, Ed?'

'I don't have one, Noreen.'

'You're not married?'

'No. There's only me.' I gulp down the last of my glass. 'And Mother.'

'Oh? Where is she? Would she like to hear the good news about Jesus?'

'She's... away.' Noreen's slip back into professional mode irritates me.

'You're not spending Christmas together?'

'No. We don't tend to.'

'Ed?'

'Yes, Noreen?'

'You're not...'

I jump in, hackles raised. 'Gay?' A poof? Queer? It's an assumption I've suffered a million times.

Noreen looks shocked. 'I was going to say lonely.'

My ego deflates. My righteous anger hisses out of me. 'Sorry, it's just I'm tired of people... Oh well, never mind. What did you want to know?'

'I asked you if you were lonely, Ed?'

I examine my fingernails. 'Perhaps a little. I'm... cautious. Yes, cautious. I don't like getting my heart bruised.'

Noreen puts her nearly untouched glass down, rises and tucks the folio under her arm again.

'Well, thank you, Ed. But it's time for me to finish off the Lord's work.'

'Why don't you go home, Noreen? Surely Jesus can manage without you for just one night? Besides, it's his birthday.'

She smiles, but it hides nothing. 'Christmas is nothing but a pagan festival. We don't celebrate it at our church.'

'Your church sounds a bundle of laughs.'

I regret this immediately, as I watch Noreen's face close up against me. 'They've been very good to me. Ever since David...'

I'm up on my feet before she can finish.

'Listen, let's not do this.'

'What?'

'Swap sad stories. I think, Noreen, our moment has passed. Happy Christmas.'

Noreen rises, brushing away tears. Then she reaches out and cups my cheek. It's so long since someone touched me, but all I can think about is how my bladder feels like a hard round stone. I break away.

'You're not so bad, Ed.'

'Reckon I might survive the end of the world?'

'I'll put in a good word for you.'

'Thanks.' I'm hopping from foot to foot now, cringing with pain. 'Just stay there a minute. I have to go to the loo and then I'll see you out.'

'It's okay. I think I can find my way to the door.'

'No, no. I insist. I'm your host. Anyway, I have to make sure you don't steal the family silver.'

She laughs and sits back down again. I hobble away to relieve my discomfort.

In the kitchen, I pour myself some water and open my hamper. Perhaps Noreen would like a bite to eat. It would make a good apology. But I have to insist that she doesn't tell me anything about her husband. The last thing I want is her leaving me maudlin.

'Noreen? Do you want a sandwich or some cake or something? Noreen? Noreen?'

The front door clicks shut. I crumple against

the kitchen wall.

When I finally confront my empty living room, I find two things. The first is another copy of Noreen's leaflet. I snatch it up, contemplate it for a moment and then tear up the hateful publication into little pieces that the fire makes short work of.

The second is a note on a torn-out diary page: PHONE YOUR MOTHER.

I sink down, staring at Noreen's careful, certain hand. Then I reach for the phone. There are only a few places that Mum's likely to be. I keep their numbers in the back of my address book. Just in case.

I'll do it in a minute. Five minutes. Ten, at the very most. It's only half-nine. And how long does it take to say 'Happy Christmas'?

A Public Demonstration of Clairvoyance

I see the advert in my local paper, squeezed between the tale of the cat that jumped from the top floor of a block of flats without injury, and the story of Mrs Cribbins, who claims she can see the face of Jesus in the watermark on her twenty pound note.

'A Public Demonstration of Clairvoyance by Paul Frizell', an apparently internationally-acclaimed medium. Attached to his name is the legend, 'As seen on TV'.

If he's as seen on TV, how come I've never heard of him? If he's internationally acclaimed, why is he appearing in a dump like my hometown?

Still, it might be fun. I ring Mum up to see if she wants to come along. She goes through bouts of wanting to communicate with the other side, even though her religion forbids it. I explain the details to her, before she starts pontificating on something completely unrelated.

'I thought you might want to see if...' I pause to take a breath, '...if Dad came through.'

This suggestion is greeted with a silence broken only by the digital hum of the phone line.

Then Mum laughs. 'Your father? I don't think so, Claire. He never had any conversation when he was alive. Death won't have changed that.'

She laughs again and I join in, although it hurts to do so.

'I suppose you're right. Well... what about Gran?'

'What about her?'

'Haven't you ever...' I don't dare to continue. My maternal grandmother is a sacred totem, the epitome of idealised motherhood. The idea that she would deign to communicate with some second-rate medium is suspect.

Mum sighs down the phone. Not impatience. Not anger. Weariness, born from years of suppressed desire.

'I just thought... you might like to know... that she was okay.'

We pause, as if by agreement. I hear a click as Mum fiddles with her phone cord. I picture her pale face, her tightened jaw and clenched knuckles.

I will let her break this silence.

'You know what your Gran always said, Claire. She said she'd tell me everything when I was 21.' Her voice shrinks. 'Of course, she never had the chance.'

'So you'll come then?'

Mum laughs. 'Oh no. I don't think so, Claire. What would I tell the priest?'

'Don't say anything, Mum. Just don't mention it.'

'No. You go. I'm sure you've got some friends who'll enjoy it. It's probably all phooey anyway. But... if... if she does... come across, Claire... well... let me know, wont you?'

'Of course.'

The day arrives and I've said nothing to anyone else about it, not even anyone at work. Not that I'm particularly sociable. They watch any old rubbish the telly spews out. Most of the women go to book groups where, over several glasses of wine, they discuss the foibles of their husbands and children, rather than the literary merits of the latest blockbuster. My male colleagues pimp their cars, or weight-lift or fish, so I've no conversation with them either. Six years I've been in this office and I'm yet to find my niche.

I leave early for the clairvoyance evening, even though it doesn't start till eight. I have to go home and mentally prepare. I keep pushing away the momentous feeling I have, the sense that I'm about to stumble upon an important truth. I have a couple of Voddies to relax me and then go out for the early bus.

The backroom of the Rose and Crown is as bad as I remember it. It's fitted out with rows and rows of straight-backed chairs, with thin cushions clad in scuffed orange velveteen. Someone has added a 'Function Room' plate to one of the doors. It fails to lend any grandeur to a space stale with so many years of cigarette smoke and spilt beer.

A heavy-bosomed Earth Mother type takes my

fee. A tangerine pashmina hangs in voluminous folds from her shoulders. Her face and noodle hair are a similar shade. I wonder if the colour assists her vibrations.

'First time, is it?'

I'd be impressed if it wasn't for the fact that I'm the only member of the public here just now. The others obviously know not to turn up until later. And I keep pushing my bracelets up my arm and letting them jangle back down.

'Yes, I thought I'd give it a go.'

'I hope you get the answers you want,' she says, beaming at me.

For a fiver, so do I.

A medley of psychic miscreants ring the walls, offering angel therapy, palm reading, Tarot cards, and healing crystals. There are no prices on display. I fear for my purse's health.

I order a Voddy and take a table across from the doorway, cradling my drink like a treasured pet. The room starts to fill up. Notes change hands. The secrets of past, present and future are unveiled. I look on, resentful, wishing I could cross the border from cynicism to credulity.

The Angel Cards reader passes my table on the way to the loo.

'Penny for them,' he lisps at me.

I smile as mysteriously as I can manage.

'I bet you're looking for a good man, like the rest of us.'

My smile hardens until Angel Cards waltzes away with an 'Excuse Me!' expression on his face.

At five to nine, everything stops. The peddlers release their clients. Earth Mother floats in, summoning our attention. She asks us all to take a seat. I hover for a moment. This is tricky. I'm sure as hell not sitting with the trade in the back row. I steer clear of the next few rows, which are as rowdy as a hen-night. Plenty of bleached hair and cheap gold. No room for me there. Towards the front there's a sea of middle-aged beige. Here, I could catch anything from the menopause to a love of *Countdown*.

Which leaves me the front row with its single old lady inhabitant.

I'm overjoyed. It's a Biddy.

They're a dying breed. Mum and me used to go Biddy-spotting all the time. We could sniff out a heavy tweed coat half a mile away. We delighted in the cheap glitter of a paste lapel brooch. And we were inconsolable if the ensemble wasn't completed by a tartan shopping trolley and suede, fur-lined front-zipping ankle boots. Invariably, our quarries shopped for ham shanks and split peas to make rib-coating broth with. In the winter they covered their blue rinses with paisley head scarves.

But they've disappeared from our streets. As the new millennium progresses, the old orders are swept away. Fashions change and Biddy coats now hang neglected in charity shops. Their brooches are worn by 'hip' teenagers in the name of irony.

I nod my head in tribute. My Biddy offers me a

smile. Her faux-crystal brooch sparkles with prisms of light.

'First time?'

I nod, unable to voice my weird anxieties.

'I've been to lots of these shows. Loads and loads. This one's a good 'un.'

'Is he? You've had messages through him?'

She smiles again, trying to distract me from the sadness that flares in her eyes.

'Oh no. I've never heard from my daughter. But it's a comfort to hear the messages that come through for others.'

'Well... maybe tonight'll be your lucky night.' I flex my toes inside my heels, cringing at my hollow reassurance. Biddy-woman gives me another sad smile and turns away.

The room dims, leaving just a single spotlight trained on the stage blocks. Earth Mother leads the applause as the main man emerges from behind us. He steps straight into the spot without blinking and the applause ratchets up.

Paul Frizell is a small man, with a long snout and two tiny jet beads for eyes. His overbite is an orthodontist's dream. His hands are matted with the same wiry black hair that's on his head and every one of his stumpy fingers is bejewelled. His stomach is beginning to stretch his velvet jacket out of shape. When he smiles, he becomes that slightly sinister relative that every family has. The one that turns up to every hatch, match and dispatch, even though no one talks to him. Or knows quite where he fits in.

His voice is low but commanding.

'Ladies and Gentlemen, thank you, thank you, thank you. You're much, much too kind.'

The applause dies down. Frizell smiles again and my blood freezes.

'Ladies and Gentlemen, the world of Spirit is drawing close to us this evening. I am the vessel, the conduit, for your communication with your loved ones. But I must beg with you, must plead, that we have absolute silence during the demonstrations, so that our messages arrive with complete clarity. They are indeed the necessary scourge of the modern age, but tonight, Ladies and Gentlemen, I would ask you to turn off your mobile phones.'

We all shift in our seats and fiddle in handbags or pockets. Except the Biddy next to me, thank God. A Biddy with a mobile would be an unfortunate departure from tradition. As if on cue, someone's phone goes off with a bone-rattling, unearthly shriek. Frizell's smile threatens to escape the bounds of his podgy face.

'Looks like they're trying to get through to you already, dear.'

The mediums laugh. The audience politely joins in. The girl who owns the mobile glows with embarrassment.

I reach into my handbag and check, for the thirteenth time, that I've switched mine to silent. I would absolutely die if something like that happened to me.

Frizell takes a deep breath, raises his hands to

shoulder height, turns his palms outwards and closes his eyes.

We wait, in silence, our own breath hushed as the medium 'falls' into a 'trance'. Mrs Biddy beside me takes a handkerchief from her pocket and dabs at the dry, pale corners of her mouth.

Frizell leaves us hanging, stretches the silence to the point of boredom. Then he breaks the thread. His eyes snap open, lifeless and unseeing. He searches the crowd like a blind man.

'Donna?'

Several women straighten up.

'My own Donna?'

Frizell drops his hands and descends into his audience. His movements are fluid and languid. His ferret face is softened with serenity.

His mark is flustered. She fans her fingers protectively over her chest.

'Darren?'

'Yes, it's me Donna. I'm alright now. How's Killer?'

Donna looks around at us, as if we're owed an explanation. This is the spirit version of the talk show. She's about to spill the beans on her whole life.

'That's our Alsatian. We've had him since he was a pup.'

People 'ah'.

Donna addresses 'Darren'. 'Killer's getting on, Darren. His back legs are going.'

Mrs Biddy wipes her eyes. I swallow a couple of times, lips and mouth dried out with anticipation.

'Donna, let him go. He'll come to me. We'll wait for you.'

At this, Donna sobs. Her friends' arms encircle her. Mr Frizell jolts out of his trance. He touches Donna's arm and whispers something in her ear. She nods and her friend leads her to the exit. Everyone rustles in their seats. Whispers ripple around the room.

Frizell returns to the stage.

'If any of you need support after hearing from your loved ones, just stop me or one of my colleagues. We're used to working with Spirit, of course. But, as you've just seen, it can be overwhelming.'

I sneak a glance at Mrs Biddy. She is nodding sagely at Frizell's words. Her knuckles blanch as her grip tightens on the straps of her shopping bag. She closes her eyes and begins to rock back and forth.

'Please let it be tonight,' she whispers repeatedly. A cross between a prayer and a mantra. Poor dear. Part of me wants to take her hand and soothe her agitation. The other part of me wants to slip out of my seat and slide unnoticed towards the exit.

Frizell dives into the nether-world once more and, for the next 20 minutes, we are treated to a string of banalities from beyond the grave. So many names and obscure details. That blue looks good in the kitchen... Have a look in the trinket box at the back of the wardrobe... Mrs Thing's out of hospital today, go round and see her tomorrow...

In a way it's nice. It cools the edge of my scepticism. How many profound conversations do I have in the course of everyday life? Why should chit-chat from beyond the grave suddenly be so... grave?

I smile to myself at my own little joke. The Voddies are working their magic. I think Mum would have hated this though. She was probably right to stay at home.

Mrs Biddy's rocking now. Not a great deal, but enough to make her chair squeak. Her eyes are squeezed shut and she's twisted her hanky to knots. Won't the Spirits take pity on her? Won't Frizell reward her years of devotion? A good con-artist satisfies his most vulnerable customer because their gratitude is priceless. But Frizell hasn't even noticed Mrs Biddy. Neither has anyone else. Maybe Biddies haven't died out after all. Maybe we've just stopped noticing them. Even Mum refused to go Biddy-spotting once she turned 55, in case she started looking at them for style tips.

Frizell announces that he's about to break. This is crunch time for my deranged granny. She flips up out of her seat and bounds up onto the stage, knocking Frizell to the ground as she does so.

The audience gasp with horror. A couple of his colleagues race to help him up. Mrs Biddy is now a quivering mass. She's having some kind of fit. This is awful. Why isn't anyone doing anything?

Why are they so concerned for Frizell? She throws her head back and lets out a low, sinister moan. Frizell cuts through her pompously.

I'm right. She is invisible.

'Ladies and Gentlemen, there is no cause for alarm. Sometimes Spirit energy is so very, very strong. But I'm unharmed. And I'll return after the break.'

The audience break into applause. What's wrong with him? Can't he see this woman needs some help? What's wrong with us that we'd rather ignore the mental health problems of an elderly woman than give up our pretence that the dead are communicating with us?

I push my bracelets up my arm, trying to decide what to do. The old woman opens her eyes and points a crooked finger at me. 'Tell her...'

Oh God, I don't want to be here any longer. I look around me, but no one seems concerned. They're acting like nothing is happening, heading for the bar or gossiping about what's taken place so far this evening.

I rise now and step up to the platform, vaguely intent on grabbing Mrs Biddy's hand and dragging her back to her chair. There must be a number, someone I can call. Someone I can get to pick her up, take her home, stay with her as this latest breakdown develops.

'Ssh, it's okay. Why don't we go and sit down? I'll get you a glass of water. Or we could go outside, get some fresh air?'

I try to close my fingers around hers but my

judgement is off. She evades my attempts.

'You tell her...'

I realise I've no choice but to play along with her.

'Tell who?'

'You tell my daughter... My Joanie...'

Oh Christ. Oh Mum! I don't want to hear this. I really don't want to hear this.

'Come on down now, stop being so silly.'

I'm aware of a little crowd behind me. God knows what I look like, waving my hands into empty space, having a conversation with someone only I can see.

And now the tears roll from my eyes as I hear the message my Mum has longed for all her life.

'Tell my Joan. Tell her I'm sorry.' I have never seen such sadness. My heart is about to break. And I know what she wants to say. I know the years of frustration that have led to this moment.

Mrs Biddy – I should really call her Gran – begins: 'I'm sorry I never got to tell her...'

'I know, Gran, I know. You don't have to finish.'

'...all the things I was saving until she was 21.'

She smiles and leans in to me, imparting the knowledge that my Mum never received.

My vision narrows to an escape route. I find a clear path to the ladies'. Inside the cubicle, I let go of my twisted stomach.

Vodka and fish pie aren't so great regurgitated.

A few days later, Mum phones. 'So how did it go then?'

'How did what go, Mum?'

She laughs. 'The Spirit thing, silly.'

'Oh, pretty dull actually.'

'Oh.'

'I wouldn't go again.'

'Wouldn't you, Claire?' There's a pause. I wince and hold my breath for the question.

'I take it nobody we... knew... came through?'

I cross my fingers and my toes. 'No, no one we knew made an appearance.'

'Oh.'

Mum fishes around for something to smooth over her disappointment. 'I think I'll get my hair done.'

'Good. Go to that really nice place in town and I'll pay for it.'

Guilt money.

'That's very kind of you. Thanks, Claire. See you next week?'

'Hm.'

She puts the phone down. I sigh with relief and close my eyes. It's easier to lie to her than I thought. Today. But then there's all the other days. And the years and years... keeping secrets gives me heartburn.

'Mum, I lied. Mum, Gran really did come through. And the thing you were going to be told, when you were 21? Well, Mum, it appears... I mean, if you can trust these things... if that was really Gran coming through to me... then... well... she said, she said... that... you were... adopted...'

Business Trip

Friday

I wake when your alarm goes off and lie there, on the edge of dreams, listening to you run the shower for ages. You pad back along the landing and must dress quickly, because the next thing I know, this room is filled with your new after-shave. I certainly won't miss it. It's too complex for me. I prefer simple scents like musk and leather, things you tell me are out of fashion.

You catch sight of yourself in the mirror and stop to smooth down your hair and examine your skin. I can't remember the last time you took so much pride in your appearance. Probably before we were married.

Then you pick up your hold-all and stuff it full of clothes. I almost want to get out of bed and fold them properly for you. Instead, I dig my finger-tips and toes into the mattress.

On top of this mess goes the photo of your Mum and Dad, in the silver frame I bought you last Christmas. I'll miss it. I love your Mum and Dad. That's why I'm leaving it up to you to tell them.

You go squeaking back and forth, across the floorboards you insisted on stripping back and sanding. I wanted to keep the carpet, but you wouldn't have it. The hours we rowed over it! I won't miss having to try and be a UN negotiator in my own home.

Your footsteps stop and I think you're about to sneak out without saying goodbye, that that's the sort of coward you really are.

I don't expect the kiss on the forehead.

'Is that you off then?' I ask, as brightly as I can manage.

'Yep. See you, Julia.'

It's not much of a goodbye, is it?

Once you press the door closed I roll over and attempt sleep. It comes in fits and starts, one ear open for your grovelling return.

I go into work for the afternoon, trying to forget the empty house waiting for me this evening. Carla has already left for the weekend. Did you plan it this way?

There's a post-it on my desk, telling me that she'll see me on Tuesday. That we need to talk.

Have you put her up to this? Do you harbour fantasies of us all getting on together? Of good old Jules strapping on her brave face? You know me better than that, don't you?

There's something different in the office. Whispered conversations which break abruptly whenever I appear. Someone asks me what I'm doing over the weekend. I tell them 'nothing in particular'.

On the way home I get a pain in my back and a strange fluttery feeling in my stomach. I take myself to bed for an hour, hoping it will wear off. I lie completely still, afraid to move. Bored, with only my pain for company, I get up and brave it out on the sofa watching all the compulsively crap TV you hate. Eventually the pain and the butterflies subside, without developing into anything more serious.

I cradle the phone in my lap until bedtime. It really does need replacing. The cord is all tangled up and several of the numbers have worn away. You'd talked about getting a sleek digital cordless one. I don't suppose there's any need for it now. You don't need to have your conversations in private any more.

You don't phone. You don't rush back to say you've changed your mind.

Saturday

A big fat weekend of nothing in particular planned. I'm grateful to get out of bed. It's definitely expanded in the night. And, yes, I miss your warmth. Better to be up, in the kitchen filling the mini-cafetiere, finally getting the news section of The Guardian to read first, running a bath I intend to linger in for an hour, without you banging on the door in the middle of it.

After that, I have a mad half hour of wandering about the house, going from room to room, looking for stuff you've left behind. Trouble is, in all the years we've been together, apart from clothes and ornaments, most of the things in the house are ours. Not yours. Not mine. Ours. Now what do I do with them?

Helen comes to my rescue by ringing me at eleven o'clock. We arrange to meet in a café on the Quayside. It's extremely busy. We wait twenty minutes for someone to take our order, filling the time by exchanging our news.

'How's Mark? Enjoying the conference?'

'Hmm. Sort of. You know how these things are.'

She laughs loudly and tells me how Barry spends so much of his time drinking when he's away that he's ill and miserable for a week afterwards. I feign concern. At least I no longer have to deal with your hangover blues.

Window-shopping is great fun. I try on a dress: a scarlet, floaty piece with a scalloped hem that stops just above the knee. The neckline plunges lower than I'd usually dare. Helen thinks it's lovely. It's definitely an extravagance, so in the end I hang it back on the rail. Things in that quarter seem a little fragile for now.

We part at the Metro station and I return home with credit card intact, content to have spent time with Helen. It's weird how marriage makes you drift away from your friends. At least, I'll have more time for them now. If they call.

The answer machine blinks at me in the hall. I replay the tape waiting to hear your apology. Instead, I get a minute of silence. I try 1471, but the number is withheld.

The evening passes slowly. I retire to bed with a book.

Sunday

It takes more effort to get out of bed this morning. I look like a gorgon, the result of a night spent in terrible dreams. The sorts of dreams that you'd laugh at if you were here to listen to me re-telling them.

The day crawls round to lunchtime. I have that strange feeling in my stomach again. I can't shake the notion that you're going to call. You must realise your mistake by now. I wait in the kitchen, slicing my toast into thin strips, trying to balance as many beans as possible on to each sliver of bread.

When I eventually finish, I wash my dishes, change into my tracksuit and go for a gentle run. Through the park, past the white goblets of the magnolia trees and the early summer bluebells. Wild garlic perfumes the air.

I'm not making much effort, coasting downhill and taking time to notice my surroundings. Everywhere everyone is in couples, even my fellow joggers. Breathless, I cut things short and return to the confines of the house.

Part of me is convinced that I can't go on like this. The other part is determined not to go under.

I phone Mum.

'How's Mark getting on, love?'

'Oh he's fine.'

'Good. You must be rattling around that house without him.'

'A bit.'

'Never mind, Julia, he'll be back soon. When did you say his conference finished?'

'I didn't. Anyway, I have to go, in case he rings.'

'Oh. Okay. See you next week, love.'

I hang up. It's a long time until morning. Things must be going well, because you don't call. Don't you know you could come back any time, as long as that's what you really want?

Monday

Never have I been so glad to get to work and spend the day in the office. No clients to harass or harangue me. I don't think I could solve their problems today. I've enough just holding on to my own life. My little mantra helps me to get a grip.

'Every day, in every way, I'm getting better and better.'

And what's so bad about today? Just me, the PC and mountains of admin. And no Carla, thank God. I don't think I could cope with her crowing, her satisfaction. Oh, I know she wouldn't do it on purpose... but women are like that. They really can't help themselves. I'd be like that, if things were different.

I throw myself into the piles of letters and reports that I have to answer or file. Absorbed by my work, I miss lunch.

Late afternoon, Tony stops by my desk. 'Julia, your mascara's run.'

'Has it?'

'You okay? You look a bit pale. Didn't see you at lunch.'

'I forgot to go.'

'Take a break then, eh? I'm knocking off early. Fancy a walk?'

I agree readily and we leave together, clocked by a number of our more prurient colleagues. Amused, I take Tony's arm.

Being away from the office is a relief. Moist, cool air blows off the river. I let Tony go a little ahead and we walk in silence, out of step with each other.

'It's hard when they go away, isn't it?' says Tony.

'Yes, I suppose it is.'

After three mouthfuls of my sandwich I rip it apart and scatter it onto the dull, choppy water for the seagulls to squabble over. Overhead, the blunt thunder of traffic moves across the bridge.

'You can get used to anything you know. Even separation.'

'Perhaps. It's early days yet.'

'Of course it is, Jules. But you know where I am, if you want to talk.'

'Thank you.'

I put my arm back through Tony's and we return to the office. He doesn't offer any other advice. I want to tell him everything, but I still don't have the words to.

Tuesday

Carla returns this morning. She looks so well, full of that barely-contained excitement, that glow that only a new relationship can bring. I take it as consolation. At least you haven't played me for months on end.

I wait, aware that she's around, my nerves jangling whenever she enters my orbit. It's the same feeling I get if I have to complain in a restaurant. It takes her nearly half an hour to reach my desk.

'Can I help you?'

Her smile widens. 'We could do with a chat, Jules, couldn't we?'

Will it change anything? Does she expect it to 'clear the air'? I don't believe she's that stupid.

Tony and I are out on client visits today. He'll drive and we'll take it in turns to work through our caseloads.

'Sorry, Carla, no can do. I'm out all day. Excuse me.'

I push past Carla on the way to the ladies'. The pain in my back, the fluttering in my stomach returned today. My period's come, almost five weeks late. I didn't tell you about that, did I? You see, Mark, I can have secrets too. In a way, given how things are, it's a relief.

What would you have done, Mark, if I'd rung you up to tell you that you were going to be a father?

I spend ten minutes in the loo, fixing my face and making sure the last of my tears have flowed.

At least for now.

Whatever I do, I mustn't get upset in front of Tony. It would just confuse things right now.

I wait in the car whilst he visits his first client. Then we drive to Mrs Houghton's. Her mobility is severely limited and she spends all her days and nights in an armchair, by the front window. Three of her grown-up children live close by, but she spends most of her time alone.

'They's embarrassed, see, by my weight. Worried they'll go same way, I'll bet. So, I watches the world from here and wonders.'

We're trying to get her a team of carers, but government restrictions mean that they can't lift her out of that chair. Her world is eighteen inches wide and twice a day her neighbour pops in to help her use a potty.

Back in the car I burst into tears. How could her family abandon the poor woman like that? Tony puts his arm round me and it's a relief to be held again. At the end of the day he invites me for a drink but I decline.

'At least let me give you a lift home.'

I know he's only being kind, but it's too much.

'A walk to the bus stop might clear my head. Thanks anyway.'

He smiles, 'If you're sure.'

I get on the bus hoping that I haven't put Tony off. That we can have that drink together some other time.

Wednesday

Why did I book a day off this week? I ring work and tell Carla I'm coming in. She laughs and tells me not to be silly. She says she'd kill for another day off, despite her long weekend. I offer to swap but she laughs even louder.

I decide to scrub the house from top to bottom. I even go through your wardrobe and empty out the last few reminders of you from in there. There's a pile of contact magazines that you neglected to mention when you were making your big confession. Is she the first, Mark? Or is she the only one who insisted on staying around, who persisted until you left me?

I know, I said I wouldn't ask questions. I'm certainly not going to ask her.

So, if the bin men look in that sack, they'll see the whole sordid trail you've left behind. Maybe I should keep these souvenirs, make a display out of them for our family and friends. So that they can see the real Mark Morren.

Later, I phone The Swan and cancel our anniversary party. We've lost the deposit, which I paid for, but I'll just add it onto my maintenance claim. I'm red-faced for a moment or two after I put down the phone. But I'm learning to toughen up, Mark. I don't really have any choice.

I sit for ages, flicking through our address book, wondering where to start telling people. I wish I hadn't agreed to this business trip story. I'll look the fool when I tell them that, even though it was you that walked away, you that gave up on our marriage, I agreed to lie for you, to give you the 'breathing space' you so desperately wanted. It stuns me that, even after such a betrayal as yours, I can agree to such an act of loyalty.

Idiot. Idiot. Idiot. There aren't enough names for my feelings about myself, for the anger I have in trusting you all this time. I take my wedding ring off and put it into a box that I find at the back of a drawer in my dressing table. I don't know what else to do with it.

The Chablis chilling in the fridge is so much more appealing than confessing the truth. I don't want to initiate the process of slicing up our connections. It's like a call to arms – announcing our split. The inevitable taking of sides, the drawn battle lines, the conflicting loyalties, we've seen it happen with too many of our friends. Now we're just the same.

No, it definitely has to be the Chablis.

Thursday

After two bottles of wine it's impossible not to sleep. Trouble is that it doesn't last. By four o'clock I'm wide awake, watching with crumpled eyes as the shadows glide across the cool white walls of my room. I get up and pace about. Start to form plans in my head. Using the Yellow Pages, I draw up a list of possible solicitors.

Now that the house is mine, I can do what I

like to cheer it up. Everything seems to need decorating. You never noticed that the doors had yellowed, or the black mark on the sitting room ceiling. And never once did you agree to hang a strip of wallpaper for me. If it couldn't be covered with emulsion, you weren't interested. There's so much to do, I don't know where to start.

I decide flowers would give the place an immediate lift. But first, I take a long, leisurely bath, frosting my body with fragrant bubbles. Then, on the stroke of 8:30, I phone the office. Carla answers breezily, keen to make me feel better about my absence. For once I use my period as an excuse. She's good at false sympathy.

'Poor you! I was hoping we'd finally catch up today, Jules. Have that talk.'

'Well, sorry, but that's the way it goes.' I pause and gather all of my courage into my chest. 'How's Mark?'

She laughs, more uncertain of herself, though. She recovers pretty well. 'He's fine.'

'Good.'

We both wait for a way to end the call. Eventually, I tell her I'll probably be back at work tomorrow and then hang up.

I unplug the phone, wrap the knotted cord around it and place it by the kitchen bin. It's worn and out-of-date. I'll go to town and buy a new one. Something in a style that I like. Perhaps one of those brass candlestick ones, to go in my new rooms with freshly papered walls.

The florist's is empty. I pick my way through buckets of gardenias, freesias and lilies and find some beautiful, blood-red roses. The assistant disappears beneath the counter and I seize the moment to select a single stem. Careful not to prick myself with the thorns, I peel off the petals and drop them to the floor.

He loves me not. He loves me not. He loves me not. He loves me not.

I crush the little pile with my heel. The vegetable scent of that little shop makes me suddenly nauseous. I scuttle towards the door, in desperate need of fresh air. Back on the street, in the sunlight, I catch my breath, free and rebellious. Lungs full, blood fiery in my veins, I wander home to make plans for my life without you.

A Little of What You Need

'The thing is, Doc, I don't know what I am anymore. What I mean to anyone.'

'You feel like you've stopped being central to your life and now you're just a walk-on role?'

Gary Knailes considered Dr Walsh's summation carefully. 'Yeah, I think that's it.'

Walsh looked at Gary slant-ways and smiled. 'I'm not surprised you feel this way, Mr Knailes. Given what you've been through, I'm sure I'd feel the same.'

'Thank you, doctor.' Gary tried to hide the irritation in his voice. Sympathy was all right, but what he needed were answers, solutions. Before Maxine walked out, taking Chelsea with her.

'So, are there any pills you can give me, Doc? To cheer me up and that?'

'I think, Mr Knailes, that prescriptions are my department. But pills, in this instance, I don't think are the solution. You have mild depression. And I'd like you to see somebody for it.'

'See someone?'

Walsh reached across to his card index. He flicked through until he found the information he wanted. He passed it to Gary.

'I can't afford this, Doc. It's private isn't it?'

'In the main, Mr Knailes, but they do some

NHS work, with patients who they feel will benefit. Their methods are somewhat unorthodox, but they get some remarkable results.'

Gary shrugged. He wasn't convinced, but he didn't feel in a position to argue with a man of Dr Walsh's years and experience.

'I'll make a referral for you, Mr Knailes. You should hear from them within a month. And, if you are to make the best of this, if you are to ensure your recovery, Mr Knailes, you must do exactly as your therapist requires. Do you understand?'

Gary nodded. The card was still between his fingers. The gold and silver logo seemed a world away from what he'd expected to happen. He couldn't tell how Maxine was going to react.

He rose from his seat and made his way to the door, then hesitated. 'Couldn't I just talk to you, Doc? Wouldn't that get me better?'

The doctor coughed and smiled as if Gary had made a mildly amusing joke. 'Look around my waiting room, Mr Knailes. Then tell me if I have the time to give you the attention that you need.'

Gary winced as several toddlers screamed in chorus.

'Right. The Wentworth Clinic it is then.'

Maxine didn't go mad, like he expected. Instead, she put Chelsea to bed early and made Gary his favourite tea of scampi, chips and onion rings. Afterwards, she washed up while he watched the European cup tie on Sky Sports. Maxine brought him a beer.

'You know, this Wentworth clinic sounds really posh. You better get a new suit, Gary.'

'A new suit?'

'Well, I don't want you making a show of me, of us. Just cos you've got depression, doesn't mean you have to let yourself go, does it?'

'Can we talk about this another time?'

'And I'll pop down to the Social for you tomorrow. Pick up some forms for your incapacity.'

Gary frowned at her. 'I'm not sick. I'm just not very happy, all right?'

'Yeah, but you can get money off the Social for it. Loads more than Dole. Wouldn't harm just to pick the forms up, would it?'

To keep the peace, Gary agreed. Maxine brought him another can.

At bedtime, Maxine spent longer in the bathroom than normal. Gary was hopeful, until she climbed into bed, turned out the light and kissed him once on the cheek. He sidled up to her, but her nightie was firmly tucked in around her legs and when he kissed her neck she told him to 'Give over.'

Sleep was shattered, as usual, by Chelsea bellowing through the house at 3 am. Another one of her night terrors. Maxine got up to tend to her, while Gary made room in the bed for the two of them, by clinging to the edge of it.

The appointment letter appeared swiftly, printed on thick, watermarked paper. He was given only a week's notice, which seemed unfair, given that the clinic was a fair hike away. A train and two buses it amounted to, but Maxine said she'd pay all of his fares, as long as Gary went.

'I'm not getting a new suit, though. The one I've got'll do. If that's what you wear to counselling.'

It had taken Gary a while to refer to his treatment by its proper name.

'It's just talking and that, Maxi, isn't it? Like we do.' Like we used to do, before Chelsea came along, he wanted to add. He didn't, because it felt like treachery to his beloved daughter; like treachery to Maxine's mothering.

'It's more than just passing the time of day, Gary. It's about telling someone how you feel.'

'I love you,' Gary said, trying to catch Maxine in an embrace. She slipped out of his reach and walked out of the room.

'Where you going?'

'Chelsea's crying.'

Gary flopped down into an armchair and hugged himself.

The morning of his first appointment, Gary studied himself in the mirror. He looked a prat in a green shirt with a grey and pink tie. He looked a prat in a suit, which is why he dreaded weddings, christenings and funerals. Maxine tightened the knot against his throat.

'You look dead handsome.' She kissed him on the cheek, but even this wasn't enough to convince him.

'You do love me, don't you, Maxi?'

'Course I do. Why?

Gary sat down on the bed. 'Cos I'm not going.'

Maxine folded her arms across her chest. 'You have to. It's the only hope we've got.'

He took hold of her hands and pulled her towards him. She softened a little.

'How much do you love me?'

She looked over his shoulder to avoid his scrutiny. 'You're my everything, Gary. You know that.'

Her lie lent him the strength to comb his hair, kiss her on the cheek and set off for his appointment.

A convoluted walk followed his two buses and a train ride. The route suggested to him by the Clinic took Gary round the outskirts of the town and through a trading estate, where men loaded wagons in their blue overalls. It seemed particularly cruel to him, to have to pass these industrious scenes. Gary would have happily stripped off his suit and walked round in his boxers for the chance of a day's work. Instead, he noticed that the men looked him up and down with suspicion, as if he was out of place.

Gary arrived at the Wentworth Clinic with five minutes to spare. If he'd felt out of place before, he seemed doubly so here. The tinted glass and steel cube before him looked more at home in New York than nestled among a load of factories and warehouses.

It took Gary three attempts to discover the door, so he was red-faced and flustered by the time he made himself known to the dark-haired girl manning the conch-shaped reception desk.

'Gary Knailes? Mr Merchant, your therapist, will be down to see you in a moment. While you wait, can I take a credit card payment from you?'

'No. No. I'm NHS.'

The receptionist checked her screen. 'I do apologise, so you are. Please take a seat then.'

She pointed to a chair which was almost see-through, moulded from a single piece of toughened Perspex. Gary perched himself on the edge, afraid what disasters further commitment might bring.

All his instincts told him to flee. He gasped for breath like a landed cod.

Above his head rose a vast atrium, smoked glass boxes lining its sides. These, he assumed, were the pigeon holes where the therapists worked. Gary raised his head, fighting dizzying nausea and shortness of breath to watch the clouds scud across the glass ceiling. He wondered if their window cleaners were paid a special rate, given the scale of the job.

He wondered if they were looking for staff.

It was not the peaceful oasis he was expecting. Every footstep rang on the marble flooring, though its perpetrator went unseen. The lift whirred and sighed constantly. Phones buzzed. Printers and faxes squeaked and chattered, churning out sheet after sheet of information and advice.

Gary began to think he'd been forgotten about when the lift doors opened and a giant in a navy suit strode towards him. Gary rose instinctively, but wished he hadn't because the man's presence was as over-powering as the building's. Perhaps he was developing vertigo.

'Gary Knailes?' A meat-plate of a hand was thrust into his line of vision.

Gary's own hand was dwarfed in it, but the giant's touch was as gentle as Maxine's once had been.

'I'm Clive Merchant. Do follow me.'

It wasn't more than three hundred yards to the lift, but Merchant's stride was so immense that Gary was breathless as the lift doors closed behind him.

'I'm sorry. I tend to forget that I have certain advantages over others.'

Gary smiled in answer, mesmerised by both the man's physical presence and his easy self-confidence.

'Harold Walsh referred you to me, didn't he?'

For a moment the name didn't register with Gary and then he mumbled a 'yes.'

'Did he explain about our methods here? Or my method, in particular?'

Gary shook his head. Dr Walsh had said so little about the Wentworth Clinic and now he knew why.

'Well, all we ask, Mr Knailes, is that you re-main open-minded. Everything new takes a little time to get used to.'

Gary was going to ask what he was going to have to get used to, but his stomach was impersonating a washing-machine on fast spin. The air in the lift grew stale as the tinny hum of an angry, trapped, insect sounded. Gary tapped his trouser pocket, though he knew his mobile was switched off. Maxine had made him check four times before he left the house. Merchant fished out of his pocket what Gary assumed was a Blackberry, although he could see no resemblance between it and its namesake. He watched as the therapist's huge digits deftly pressed a number of buttons to calm the agitated gadget. When he'd finished, Merchant looked over and smiled, pulling at his shirt cuffs, where circular silver links glinted.

The lift released them and Merchant led the way, at a much slower pace, to his consulting room, which was bigger than Gary expected. Only two of its walls were made of glass. Instinctively, he moved towards the cream-painted plasterboard, relieved at the temporary escape from reflective and glossy surfaces.

Furniture was sparse. A desk, turned towards the outer wall, presumably to make the best of the views, a huge padded black leather office chair, a white chaise lounge with a baby blue blanket folded on it, a plastic veneered table and a simple, straight-backed chair which Merchant now offered to Gary, who sat obediently, as if he was in the headmaster's office ready for scolding.

'I don't know what your expectations of therapy are Gary, but you'll find I have my own particular ways. In a moment, I will set this clock, so that it alerts us when your hour is up. Firstly, I want you to slip off your shoes, jacket and tie and place them over there.'

Merchant pointed to a coat rack, where Gary obediently hung his things. He took particular care to place his shoes together on the floor. It wasn't a careless sort of room.

'Good. Now the clock.' Merchant fiddled with it for a moment and then replaced it on the desk.

The two men stood opposite each other in their socks and open shirts. Merchant crooked his neck to avoid scraping his head on the ceiling.

'I want you to shake out your limbs, Gary, like this, until they feel floppy.' He mirrored the giant's wild, flailing, movements until Gary, despite his embarrassment, began to relax.

'Now, when you're ready, I want you to go over to the couch and wait for me. I'll join you there in a second. Then I'll wrap you in the blanket...'

'Wrap me in the blanket?'

'Trust me, Gary, it's an essential part of the therapy.'

'But...this is crazy...this is mad.'

'If I had fifty pounds for every time a patient's said that to me, I'd be incredibly rich right now. Just trust me, please. In a minute, I will wrap you in a blanket and we'll spend the next hour in silence. You'll go back to a state where you had no worries. Back to a time when you couldn't articulate them.'

Gary shook his head. 'I thought talking was

what I was sent here for.'

Merchant smiled. 'Sometimes, Gary, talking is the worst thing you can possibly do.'

He was newborn, with no awareness of how shitty the world could be. He was newborn, warm and safe within the huge, soft blanket, Merchant's arms locked around him like a safety belt.

'I have never...' Gary began to speak, but his throat was rusted with silence and Merchant placed a huge finger on his lips anyway and pointed to the clock.

When the hour was over, Merchant unwrapped him and Gary felt a rush of rejection. He dressed in silence and sped out the door. He was waiting for the lift when Merchant loomed down on him.

'Your next appointment. See you then.'

Gary took the card, and turned away. When he looked back as he got into the lift, Merchant was gone.

Gary was in shock. He'd let a man, a giant, wrap him in a blanket and hold him for an hour. And the difficult part was that he'd enjoyed it. The combination of the blanket and the silence had induced a state of profound calm, the like of which he'd not felt for years. He pictured himself co-cooned in the blanket, with Merchant encircling him.

If anyone ever found out...

'How was it?' Maxine greeted him with Chelsea

wedged on her hip.

Gary coloured and shrugged. 'Okay. Don't know if I'm going back though.'

'What? Why?'

'I'm not sure it's my sort of thing, you know.'

'Gary, we agreed!'

He held his hands up. 'I know we did, Maxi, I know. But this therapy thing, it's just not...natural.'

She didn't answer straight away. Instead, she dumped Chelsea on Gary's knee. The little one immediately started crying. Gary tried to shush her, but she began to scream. Maxine slammed the front door behind her.

'Maxine! MAXINE. She needs you.'

Through the front window, Gary watched his wife shrug and set off down the street. Chelsea wailed harder, until the neighbours banged on the wall. Gary sniffed at her nappy, but it was clean. He tried to give her a dummy, but this made her worse. The remains of her dinner lay on an orange plastic plate in the kitchen.

'If I had to eat that sloppy gunk, I'd cry too,' Gary said.

His apology failed to pacify his daughter, so Gary was forced to resort to something he wasn't sure would work. He carried Chelsea up the stairs and searched in the airing cupboard until he found one of the old woollen blankets they kept in case the heating broke down. With her still threatening to split his ear-drums, he wrapped his unhappy daughter in the blanket and held her tight. Within minutes she was fast asleep.

Maxine was so delighted when Gary announced he'd decided to give counselling another go that she didn't insist on him wearing his suit. He felt much more comfortable in jeans and sweatshirt. He also knew what to expect, but that didn't stop a tidal wave rising in his guts as he neared the clinic.

This morning he found his way in immediately. The door was propped open and the lobby was cluttered with boxes of paperwork. Each one was labelled in marker pen, *C. Merchant*.

Gary approached reception. 'I'm here to see Mr Merchant.'

The receptionist's smile died. 'Oh. Mr Knailes? If you'd just like to follow me.'

'Is something wrong?'

'Come this way, please.'

She led him past the conch-shaped desk and into a mirrored corridor. At the far end, was an office. The receptionist knocked once and then led him straight in.

'Mr Knailes?'

Gary's hand was shook limply by a robust balding man, the lower half of his face swamped by a salt and pepper moustache. He reminded Gary of a walrus.

'I'm the director of the clinic, Piers Wentworth. Would you like to take a seat?'

'No, I'd rather stand. I have an appointment with Mr Merchant in a minute.'

Wentworth smiled. 'I'm afraid your appointment has been cancelled.'

'What? Do you know how long it's taken me to get here? How much I've spent on buses and trains?'

Wentworth looked as if he couldn't care less. 'Please calm down, Mr Knailes. The fact of the matter is Mr Merchant isn't working for us any longer.'

'Since when?'

Wentworth straightened the lapels of his jacket. 'All of our staff undergo rigorous checks and monitoring, in order to protect our clients. There are some deeply unscrupulous people out there, Mr Knailes.'

'I know. But Clive Merchant isn't one of them.'

'I'm afraid that isn't the case, Mr Knailes. It seems that not only are Mr Merchant's methods highly unorthodox...'

'Does that matter if it works? I've only been to one session with him and I'm already starting to feel better.'

'I'm glad to hear that, Mr Knailes, but it changes nothing. Mr Merchant's qualifications don't check out. They're the sort of thing that can be bought over the Internet for a very small sum of money. He is not a qualified therapist.'

'In that case, Mr Wentworth, he's a bloody genius.'

Six months passed. Gary and Maxine fell apart. There were no fights or recriminations. He just came home from the job centre one day and found she'd packed her and Chelsea's things.

Gary allowed himself a few tears and then rang Maxine's mum to ask about seeing Chelsea. Maxine came to the phone.

'Whenever you want Gary. There's no one else. And you're a good dad. Especially that blanket thing you do. You'll have to show me sometime. I don't seem to have the knack. I've tried, but she squeals all the more when I do it.'

'I'm not surprised. It's something you need to have experienced.'

'What's that, Gary?'

'Doesn't matter. Maxi, I'm sorry, you know.'

'I'm sorry too, Gary. But it's not going to change. We're not going to change.'

'No, maybe not.'

Gary put down the phone and warmed some tinned curry and packet rice for his tea. He ate it on a tray in the living room, watching the sports round-up on the local news. He washed his dishes and went for an early night. He had a job interview the next morning. Warehouseman on a trading estate.

That night, he dreamt of a giant blue blanket and the largest pair of hands in the universe. He woke up and wondered where Merchant was plying his therapy now.

Happy Birthday, Son

Barbara wakes with a start, from unkind dreams. She's hugging herself and her eyes sting, as if she's spent the night crying.

She considers burying her head under the duvet and remaining there all day, but then remembers it's her day to visit John. Barbara bolts up, wrapping her pink robe around her. There's so much to do.

Fluffy appears with a present between his jaws. A bird this time, a tiny sparrow, mercifully dead and only slightly chewed. Fluffy deposits his treasure on her Chinese rug, and waits for her to inspect and approve, mewing proudly and standing to attention by the corpse.

'What a good boy!' She rubs behind his left ear, eliciting delicious purrs. Satisfied, Fluffy trots away, his tail aloft in a furred question mark.

Barbara kneels beside the wasted bird. She scoops it up into a food bag and places it to one side. Before her hair appointment she has the house to clean and the cake to make.

There's a mouse waiting for her in the bathroom, its tiny paws raised in surrender. She wraps the rodent in another food bag and places it on the toilet cistern, until she's finished her shower. She changes into cords and a t-shirt, her working gear, so that her dress will remain unspoilt for this afternoon.

In the kitchen, Barbara gathers all her ingredients together. She rifles through her treats cupboard for some Smarties and then remembers that she ate them all last week, during a repeat of Inspector Morse. Barbara grabs some change and her keys and hurries down to the newsagent.

'Morning Barbara. What can I get you?'

'A *Daily Mail* and a tube of Smarties, please.'

Wilf gives her a concerned smile. 'That time of year again, is it?' He sucks air in over his teeth. 'Comes round quickly, doesn't it?'

Barbara nods, unable to find her voice. She doesn't want to cry. Today should be a celebration. She takes her change, and Wilf wishes her a good day.

Back at home, she puts the Smarties on the kitchen bench and her paper by her bed for this evening. She mixes her cake batter and puts it in the fridge. Then she greases the tins she needs and lights the oven.

Her floor-cleaning quickly descends into farce, as Fluffy crashes through his door and catches sight of the mop. He pounces on the many-tentacled creature, catching as many strings as he can between his claws, while the free ones tantalise him into a fury.

'Fluffy, get off.'

He grips harder. Barbara makes a mighty effort and pulls him across the floor. He yowls. She begins to laugh, despite her anger. Eventually she gives up, lets the mop-shank fall, and gives into a mixture of ringing, hiccupping laughter and great, globular tears.

Fluffy comes to her, nestling between her splayed legs. He finds her hand and licks it.

'Thanks boy.'

At the salon, Damian massages her scalp, while chatting in his soothing voice.

'How are you today?'

Her voice is surprisingly steady. 'Fine. Just a shampoo and a trim, please.'

She sounds like her mother. Barbara digs her fingernails into the soft leather of the chair.

'Busy day?'

Barbara nods. 'Yes.' She tries to add something, but her thoughts dry up.

Damian smiles, lifting her hair on his scissors, to gauge the length of the trim she requires. 'Why don't we try some colour in this, Miss Daniels?'

'Colour?'

'Yes, something to warm it up. Some copper highlights perhaps. And have you thought about having it layered?'

Barbara raises her eyes and manages to face her own reflection. It would be nice to have something different... to be someone different.

'What do you think? Colour?'

She comes to a decision. 'I don't think I've the time for that. I'm visiting my son this afternoon. And I'm doing some baking for him. I have to get back.'

And she's got a budget to think of.

'Oh, come on, Miss Daniels. It won't take long. And you'd suit it, honestly.'

'No. No, I don't think so. I haven't the time. It's my son's birthday, you see.'

'Oh okay. I just thought... How old is he?'

There is an easy answer to this. 'Thirty-five. He's thirty-five.'

Damian asks no more questions. He cuts her hair in silence. Barbara wonders whether she should have taken the chance, whether he's annoyed with her for not being adventurous.

'There you go.' Damian waits for her approval. He looks blankly at her. She's sure he's upset. Damian shows her the back of her head in the mirror. Barbara nods and mumbles a thank you, though she can hardly see any difference. That's what she deserves. Damian lowers the chair and removes the cape, not bothering too much about the snipped hair flying into Barbara's face. When he's finished, Damian directs her to the junior behind the counter so that Barbara can settle up.

The girl's blonde-and-orange hair is spiked up, like the crest of a cockatoo. Barbara gives an involuntary shake of the head. She's trying to picture herself coiffed something like this. It makes her want to giggle.

The girl rings up the price and Barbara fumbles with the clasp on her bag, desperate to get to her purse and be gone. The bag springs open and out drop two mice, their carcasses rolling to a stop

131

at the junior's feet.

She shrieks.

'I'm sorry. I'm so sorry.' Barbara repeats herself over and over as the girl continues to scream and Damien rushes over to see what the problem is. Eventually, he calms the girl down and leaves Barbara to scoop the corpses back into her bag and scuttle out the shop. She leaves behind a much larger tip than she intended.

Barbara returns to an empty house. Fluffy is off foraging somewhere. Good! She will swing for him. It took months for her to pluck up the courage to go to Split Enz. And now she can't go back. Now she'll be known as 'The Mouse Lady'. Where will she go next?

Thank God, the cake is perfect. Her sponges have risen beautifully and are golden on the top. The house is full of the cake's comforting smell. Barbara turns the two rounds onto a cooling rack and begins to make the icing.

It's the same every year. Fondant for the top and butter-cream for the centre. The butter-cream is spread across a generous layer of raspberry jam.

Barbara spells John's name out in Smarties across the top of the icing. When she's finished, she pops the blue Smarties back into the tube. These are hers, at John's insistence. Blue Smarties are Mum's Smarties.

There's a bus soon. Barbara stoops to find a suitable tin among the chaos of her below the sink cupboard. The cake will go in there, when the icing's set and then into her blue shopping bag.

Not long now.

They don't talk enough. It's another way she rations herself. It must be easier if you have more children, if you have to share your love around. Barbara has only ever had John to cling to.

The sun's brilliant today, whereas last year it poured. This year the cake won't dissolve in the rain, the rain won't run down her nose and mingle with her tears.

Today is a good day. It makes her smile. She hopes that John smiles too.

Walking up the cemetery's central avenue, under the shade of the chestnut trees, Barbara feels fresh hope. This will be a good year. The cake will be perfect. And she has enough gifts for him. She won't leave him this year thinking she's let him down.

She gave him just a plain, polished stone. No photograph, like you see on so many now. Barbara couldn't bear to share him, to put him on display like that, even though he was the most beautiful boy you could hope for with white-blond hair and huge green eyes.

At ten, he rode around on his bike, fearless, chasing the other kids in their neighbourhood.

At fifteen, his passion was nature, wildlife. Especially mice and birds. The ones that no-one thinks are important, Mum.

At twenty-five, Barbara was cradling his wasted body in her arms, afraid to move in case she hurt him. When she sees representations of Michaelangelo's Pieta – on TV or in newspapers – Barbara thinks, that's me and him. That last time in the hospice. She watched him close his eyes and whispered how much she loved him.

There are no extra touches on John's grave. No teddy bears, fairies or angels. Over the years of her pilgrimage, things have changed dramatically here. Now there are always birthday cards or Christmas cards by headstones. Some people have enclosed their loved one's plots with picket fencing and 'planted' them over with plastic roses and children's windmills, garish flowers that whirl furiously in the breeze.

No, John's grave is restrained, dignified, with its simple flower urn. Sometimes Barbara brings flowers, sometimes not. If she does, she brings bronze chrysanthemums because they seem like masculine flowers. But mostly she doesn't bother, because she hates coming back to withered blooms and knotted grey stems.

Everyone has advised her not to come more often. It took her a while, but she cut down. Once a week, once a month, once every six months, once a year.

But she doesn't want him ever to be alone, which is why she has her special gifts in her handbag. Never mind cockatoo-haired juniors or snotty stylists. John shall have his gifts.

Barbara smoothes out a patch of grass, sits down heavily and opens the tin. She cuts a sliver of cake and begins to nibble on it. The rest she'll empty out onto the lake in the park. The ducks are always appreciative.

Silently she empties out her little parcels of dead mice and birds, arranging them neatly across his grave.

'Happy birthday, Son.'

Suburbia

A quarter to five. They've made it on time. Tariq, Harry's boss, is just getting the Pizza Pick-Up ready for opening. Harry and Midge watch as he lowers chairs from tables, switches the ovens on and flips the 'closed' sign to open.

Midge takes a grubby handkerchief from her skirt pocket and dabs at the corner of Harry's mouth with it.

'What you doing?' He squirms under her touch. He hates fuss.

Midge smiles. 'It's just love, Harry. Love.'

Tariq waves hello. Midge kisses Harry on the cheek.

'See you later.'

'Promise you'll go straight home, Midge?'

'I promise, love.'

She twirls Harry round and pats his bum, gently steering him towards the door. He trots away, looking over his shoulder, blowing Midge kisses. She waves back and blushes.

Tariq unlocks the door and Harry enters. Midge watches for a moment or two as the men begin their work. Then she hoists her tapestry bag over her shoulder and makes her way to the bus station.

She has promised to go home. But her fingers

were crossed, in the pocket of her voluminous skirt, so she allows herself the indulgence of studying the route map. She strokes the purple line, tracing it all the way from the city out to the suburbs. Harry won't mind. What he doesn't know won't hurt him.

Midge joins the queue for the No. 86 and checks her watch against the digital display above her head. Both say that the 86 will be here in five minutes. Time for Midge to make a circuit of the station. If she stands still too long, everything goes loopy and she can't stand it.

Patting her bag for comfort, Midge sets off, passing shoppers laden down with M&S carriers. And one or two bookish types with their heads in weighty-looking volumes. In the far corner, young people in a uniform of black clothing and facial piercings congregate. Midge grips her bag tighter and makes a wide arc to avoid them. When she rejoins the short queue for the 86, she finds herself behind a couple of very different teenagers.

They're nice. She can tell by their smart navy blazers, trimmed with wavy gold braid. Midge should know which school it is, but it's been long enough for her to forget. Much to Midge's astonishment, the judge was right.

They have such lovely hair, this boy and girl — thickly spun gold. And their complexions are bright and clean. The girl wears a very natural-looking gloss on her lips and some eyeliner. She doesn't need anything else to draw attention to how special she is.

Midge thinks it'll be good to take a stroll along some tree-lined streets for a change. Their home – their bed-sit – is made of concrete and surrounded by concrete. The council tried to plant up some of the soil, but the pansies were ripped out as soon as they flowered.

Midge leans forward to eavesdrop.

'God, I thought he'd never shut up, Ollie.'

'Really, Bella, they should give an old pervert like that the sack.'

Midge doesn't understand their talk, but she loves their cut crystal accent. A way of talking that you'd hear on TV. She watches as they hand over their money to the driver and Midge feels suddenly embarrassed by her bulk and the huge treasure house that is her bag. It contains all her bus tickets, her collection of mints, her route map and her pizza menus. Ollie carries a violin case and has a sports bag. Bella nurses a fat file under one arm.

Midge sits opposite them. She watches out of the corner of her eye as they joke easily with each other, immersed in rapid conversation. Midge leans forward, as if their golden hair could lend her some lustre.

'Do you get the feeling you're being watched, Bella?'

'Are you surprised?'

'No, but...'

Bella places her finger on Ollie's lips. 'Ssh. Don't be rude.'

138

Ollie pulls a face at Bella's admonition.

Midge looks away, aware of the colour rising in her cheeks. She places one foot on top of another and presses down until it hurts. Harry's always telling her not to believe that she's the centre of attention. But it's hard. She can only see herself, feel herself. Even when she reaches out for Harry in the night, Midge knows that, really, she's reaching for some part of herself.

Confused by her depth of feeling, her longing to be friends with these golden kids, Midge zips open her bag and rummages around. Beneath her papers she finds one remaining finger of a chocolate biscuit. She peels back the foil from the warm chocolate and swallows the biscuit down in one go. She savours the moment of creamy sweetness on her tongue. It'll do until Harry gets home with their pizza.

As the 86 trundles out of the city, dusk begins to descend. A lone flat-stomach-and-chest jogger looms into view. Midge sucks in her own stomach in response. All her abdominal muscles tighten, but the mound of her belly remains resolute, swaddled in denim.

Across the aisle, Ollie giggles. Midge hears him say something like 'It'll take more than that', but she's perhaps mistaken. Her hearing's not what it was.

Annoyed by the pain in her tummy muscles, Midge breathes out, watching her duffle coat expand further. She's regretting that biscuit now. But she doesn't want to be sad, because this is an adventure and there are two lovely teenagers sat across from her.

The street lamps ignite and the bus windows are transformed into nuggets of amber. Seeing herself reflected in one of them, Midge is cheered to note that the glow soothes away the years, uncreasing her face and disguising the grey that streaks across her scalp.

That's better. Pleased, Midge starts humming softly to herself – an old Irish ditty about the charms of a great beauty. When Harry's had too much Stout, he often sings it to her, but Midge doesn't know all the words. The tune is enough to conjure up his warmth, the protection of his arms.

Bella and Ollie start giggling. Ollie claps out of rhythm.

'Go on 50 Cent.'

Midge shifts in her seat again and falls silent. She wishes she hadn't come now. Wishes she had gone straight home. At least she can make music there without anyone objecting.

Midge closes her eyes and pictures Harry, glowing with drink, on his knee, with his hand over hers, singing only to her in his warbling tenor. Lovely.

The children across the aisle fall silent.

Very few people get on or off for ages. Then the bus lurches to a stop and Midge opens her eyes.

Lovely streets, thinks Midge, lined with tall horse chestnuts, their branches drooping under the weight of their fruits. Large, impressive houses, set back from the road. A half-timbered mansion next to a red brick villa, ablaze with light. On the corner is a flat-roofed 1930s box of a house, its grass-green window frames providing a welcome relief from the glare of its white frontage.

The bus bell rings. Ollie and Bella get up. Ollie points the violin case at Bella and pretends to shoot it. Bella stumbles backwards, clutching her stomach and quaking with laughter.

Midge is sad to see them go. They're so happy and alive. Sometimes Midge feels like that too, but often life is a hard, heavy thing for her. Perhaps being close to them, even for just a little while, might give her a boost.

She'll never know, because the bus slows to a stop and off they get, Bella turning back to give Midge a crooked smile. At least, Midge thinks it's for her, first of all, until she looks behind her and sees a young man, not in a uniform, blushing and grinning back.

As the bus pulls away, Midge glances over at Ollie and Bella's empty seat. She's left her file there. Bella has left her pink, glittery file on the seat.

It's more than Midge can bear. She hates to be parted from anything that is hers, even for a second. Midge calls out to the bus driver, 'Wait! Wait! Wait!' The other people on the bus bury their heads in books and newspapers, or turn to the window in their daydreams. The driver calls down the bus, 'What's the matter now?'

Midge gets to her feet and swipes the file.

'Please, stop. Please, the girl... the girl... she

141

forgot her file, she needs her file.'

The driver shakes his head. Midge holds up the file as evidence and plea.

The doors hiss back open and Midge steps down onto the fine street, lined with trees. She spots the two young people ahead of her, up by the roundabout. She begins to run in her clogs, but her feet slip and slide in their baby blue casings. Her heart pounds, because she doesn't run often. She calls out.

'Bella! Ollie! You forgot this.'

Thank God she was blessed with a good pair of lungs. The teenagers turn around and she waves the file like a flag, beckoning them in, grateful they've seen her, because her stitch prevents her from moving any further.

Ollie flies towards her, arms flapping. Bella strolls like she has all the time in the world. When Ollie arrives, he pokes Midge in the tummy with the end of his violin case.

'How do you know our names?'

Midge rubs her tummy and smiles proudly. 'I listened to you talking.'

'You did what?'

Midge's pride vanishes. 'I wasn't hurting you. You were talking loudly.'

'We'll see what my sister has to say when she gets here.'

Midge holds up the file, as if it might shelter her from Bella's wrath. 'I found this on the bus. It's your sister's.'

Ollie smirks, 'I know it's my sister's. Give it to

me.'

He's small for his age and Midge is able to hold the file out of his reach. 'I'll give it to Bella.'

Ollie scowls, 'Suit yourself.'

Bella draws up beside them. She puts her hands protectively on Ollie's shoulders. 'What's going on, Ol?'

'It's that woman from the bus. She's got your file.'

Bella smiles. 'Oh you! Give it to me, then.'

This is probably what Midge should do, hand over the file, walk back to the bus stop and make her way home. But she's come this far. It's hard to give over her prize so quickly.

'Haven't you heard of *please*?' Midge is only asking a question, but it makes Bella cross. She tries to smooth things over by adding, 'I like your hair.'

Bella smiles and removes the bobble from her pony tail, so that she can shake her hair out. Midge is wide-eyed with delight. 'Beautiful.' She touches her own and is ashamed that it needs a wash, that Harry hacks at her split ends with a pair of blunt scissors.

'Please could you give me my file now? I've homework to do and...'

Midge hands over the file. Ollie and Bella walk away. A remark passes from Ollie to his sister under his breath. Midge winces, though she does not hear the words.

What other people would do is walk away as well. Midge would cross the road and find out how

143

long she has to wait for the 86 back in to town. She checks her watch and sees that it's hours until Harry finishes his shift at the Pizza Pick-up. Ollie and Bella are the only other people she's spoken to all week.

'Ow! Ow! Ow! Ow!'

Midge's call immediately has the desired effect. Bella runs back, her golden hair fanning out across her shoulders. Midge pretends her mind is the shutter for an expensive camera and snaps a shot of Bella as she covers the short distance between them.

'Are you all right?'

Midge looks, open-mouthed, at her for a moment and then remembers what she's supposed to have done. She bends over and begins rubbing her ankle.

Ollie calls from further down the street, 'Come on Bells! Mums will be worried if we don't hurry up.'

'Ssh, Ollie. Can't you see this lady's hurt?'

Midge straightens up and smiles. 'No one's called me a lady before. Apart from my Harry. Ooh! Ow!'

Bella puts arm round Midge's waist, to support her. 'Let's get you sat down and see what you've done.' They make their way to the bus shelter with Midge hobbling when she remembers to.

'Take your shoe off.'

'Why?'

'So I can look at your ankle.'

Midge doesn't really want to take her clog off.

She's had enough of this game now. She wants to go home. Bella pulls the clog away and flings it to one side.

'That's my shoe!'

'You might not need it soon.'

Midge holds her breath as Bella seizes her foot in its once-white sock. 'Tell me when it hurts.'

She pushes down on her toes, until they feel like they might snap. Midge bites her lip and whimpers.

'Sore?' There's a glint of something in Bella's eyes that Midge doesn't like. Across the road, an 86 – headed for town – crawls past. Midge wishes she was on it.

Bella pushes up on the sole of Midge's foot. 'Sore?'

There are tears in Midge's eyes, but they don't blind her to the way Bella wipes her hand on the hem of her skirt and pulls a face. 'Take off your sock, please.'

'Please, Bella, I don't want to.'

'Take off your sock. Otherwise, we can't make you better.'

Midge does as she's told, hoping that her obedience might be rewarded with an end to all of this. This is definitely the last time she goes riding the buses without Harry. This is the last time she doesn't go straight home, like she should.

Bella calls over her shoulder. 'Ollie, I think I might need some help here.'

Ollie arrives and kneels down on the other side of Midge's cold foot. 'You see, Ollie,' says his sister, ' She's got swelling. The skin's gone purple.'

Midge strains to look down. 'Are you sure?'

Ollie grins at her. 'Bella wants to be a doctor, don't you?'

The girl looks Midge in the eyes. 'Oh yes, I want to be a surgeon when I grow up. To cut people open, make things better and then stitch them back up again.'

Midge shudders. 'I don't like blood.'

'Don't you,' asks Bella, with a concerned expression on her face. 'In that case, you better look away.'

'What d'you mean?'

'Well, I can ask Ollie for a second opinion, but I think the whole foot's going to have to come off.'

'No, no, it can't. I can't.'

Midge wriggles around helplessly on the narrow plastic bus shelter seat. She tries to retrieve her sock and her clog, but they are too far out of reach. 'Help me,' she pleads with the siblings.

They answer as a chorus, 'We're trying to.'

'Ollie, hand me the knife.'

He rummages in his school bag and produces one of those huge pen-knives with every possible gadget you could want on it. Midge's eyes widen with horror. Her stomach boils with fear. The bitter taste of bile coats her tongue.

'Now, this won't hurt for long.' Bella flicks open the blade and runs her thumb across it. 'It's very sharp, which means I'll get a good, clean cut.'

'NO.'

Midge feels the cold steel against her skin.

Then warmth spreading down her thighs. A trickle of warmth that pools between her feet.

'SHE'S PISSED HERSELF. HA HA. SHE'S PISSED HERSELF.'

Bella retreats, the blade still in her hand. 'You dirty old cow. You dirty bitch. You can't even use the toilet correctly, can you?'

Ollie jigs up and down, wilder and wilder. 'She's pissed herself. She's pissed herself. She's pissed herself.'

Bella looks at Midge with disgust, her file under arm and Ollie's discarded violin in her hand. 'We only wanted to help you. And this is the way you repay us? Dirty. Dirty. Dirty old bitch.'

Midge feels soaked through with tears and urine. She watches as Ollie throws her clog up into the air. It lands with a thud on the roof of the bus shelter.

This is too much for her. She rises from the seat with her fists balled and throws her face to the sky, roaring for all she is worth.

'RUN OLLIE. SHE'S GONE COMPLETELY MAD. RUN!'

Midge waddles towards them, but they are too fast for her. Never mind. She doesn't want to touch them. She certainly doesn't want to hit them, though they deserve it. She just wants them out of the way, wants to never see them again for as long as she, and they, live.

She keeps roaring, though her throat seems to be made entirely of sandpaper now, until they have disappeared out of sight.

147

Midge puts her hand to the wet patch on her skirt and sniffs. Then she picks up her bag and reaches in to it for her phone. She finds the number and dials.

'Pizza Pick-Up? How can I help you?'

'Harry? Harry? Is that you Harry? I need you Harry, I need you to come to me now.'

Solitary Pursuits

U pon his retirement, Ernest and Lillian
enjoyed one short year of peace and re-
discovered companionship, much to their surprise
and contrary to their fears. They worked out a
routine that suited them, giving them time for
solitary pursuits as well as shared pleasures.

Then Ernest's short breath and the pain slicing
through his chest curtailed things. Lillian slipped
the travel brochures into a drawer with a sigh.
She had to steel herself, find a new strength from
within, so that they could both pass through this
crisis. She was too young to be a widow.

Mr Holman, Ernest's consultant, possessed a
light touch and reassuring manner. But the word
'bypass' rang heavily in their ears. And Lillian
noted the lines that concern drew around the
young doctor's mouth.

Ernest sat at the bottom of an NHS waiting list
for six months, until Nicholas and Alex tightened
their belts and gave their parents the cash they
needed to go private.

Suddenly, the day was upon them. Ernest's
battered green suitcase stood in the hallway.
Lillian's protests went unheeded. A new suitcase
seemed like an unnecessary expense, he told her.

She tried to cry in secret, but on that morning

her tears flowed freely. Ernest held his fear in his chest, crumpled in a fist of emotion.

'It'll be fine,' he told his wife. 'A small thing, really.' Neither of them believed him.

They insisted on driving themselves to the hospital. In the event, neither of the boys could take time off work. Lillian was glad. Any further fuss was unbearable.

She watched from the driver's mirror, as he pulled the door shut, how his gaze lingered over their house. Then he picked up his suitcase, as if they were off on one of their jaunts, and got in beside her.

Everyone was pleasant and spoke in the warm quiet tones of professional compassion. All Lillian could think of was the death and sickness that filled the place. She didn't want it claiming her husband as well.

He settled without fuss, propped up in bed, wearing his new pyjamas (one battle that he'd lost). Above his head was the sad little sign reading 'NIL BY MOUTH.' They'd normally be having a sandwich and a cup of tea at this time.

They listened intently to all Mr Holman said, although it was a script that they knew by heart. They shared a look, a telepathic moment of fear and hope.

Ernest had the easy job, explained Mr Holman. One small prick and that would be the last he knew until it was all over. His eyes twinkled and Lillian wanted to laugh at the smirk on her husband's face. She flushed with confusion and waited for her awkwardness to pass.

Next morning, they dressed Ernest in a paper gown, gaping open at the back. He was a child again, his future in the hands of strangers.

The pre-med worked its magic and Lillian stroked his hand as Ernest struggled to count to five. She tried to tell him once more, just once more, how much she loved him, but her lips were slack and disobedient. By the time she recovered their use, Ernest was unconscious.

Lillian watched him wheeled away and panicked. She ground the heels of her shoes into the floor and hugged herself, fighting the instinct to run after the medical team and rescue her husband. Eventually a nurse led her away and pressed a plastic cup, filled with tea, into her hands.

The operation began well. Mr Penrhys, Ernest's surgeon, relaxed into his Faure, and began his day of butchery. Music carried Penrhys above the violence of his task, it removed him just enough from proceedings, so that he could concentrate on the technical and ignore the meaning of his work.

As he thought himself over the worst, everything changed. The patient's pulse sank, his lifeline flattened.

Sweat beaded in fine pearls on Penrhys's forehead. Theatre entered the crash zone.

Leaving wasn't dramatic. It was just a finished model being eased out of a mould. Ernest listened to the 'pop' as his spirit slid out from the soft casing of his flesh.

Now he was a firework. A splendid rocket tearing through the fabric of existence. Soaring, not just over the rainbow, but also over the moon and under the stars.

The rushing sensation stopped abruptly, and he found himself floating in spiritual amniotic. What moved him now was not muscle and electrical impulse, but naked will. He was stripped down to this one faculty; the one facet of being he'd felt was weakest in corporeal life. Now the ether bent to his desire. He was utterly unencumbered. He laughed at the joy of absence. Absence of weight, of flesh and bone. Absence of pain.

Was this a soul? If so, religion's marketing was all wrong. They always made souls impossible burdens. But this? This was delicious!

Ernest's "laughter" increased as he turned his perception to the lifeless shell he'd just escaped.

A lump of stodgy white clay on a metal trolley. Yet, there they were, sensible well-educated people, foolishly pummelling, kneading, and firing electricity into it. His anger rose.

WHAT IS THE POINT? He bellowed. But the poor things couldn't hear him.

Or wouldn't. After all, if they knew... if they had just an inkling of what this was like, they'd have to give up. They'd unhook the machine, take off their gowns, go home early and call in sick tomorrow. The whole of Western medicine would collapse. All because the secret was out. The body was only dust. The real life was here...

Ernest wanted no more to do with them. He was sorry for their stubbornness; that they were so mistaken. Deciding to give them no more awareness, he made room for a new sensation. Which puzzled him. After all, he had nothing to sense with, nothing to see with, and nothing to think with. Yet, he was doing all these things. And now something pulled at him, at his non-existent (rather, non-corporeal – the one thing he was sure of was that he existed) centre. And it felt warm and wonderful. Like driving over a dip in the road and leaving your stomach behind. Sound filled his consciousness, a musical acceleration.

Ahead of him, the edges of physical reality blurred like a badly developed photograph. Ernest raced towards a tunnel of light, exactly as he'd once heard described on television. The tunnel consisted of the brightest light he'd ever seen, but there was no pain, no stinging or sudden blindness. It was as warm and sweet as the sound. It engulfed him. He tried to gauge how far it stretched, when he would come out of it. But, as hard as he tried, he was defeated. Accepting this, he relaxed and powered through.

Ernest was full of wonder and gentle fear. A child overwhelmed by the star-dusted universe. The ardent lover anticipating his first kiss. He tried to see the world he was out of, but it was now no more than a tiny dot, finally in its rightful place.

Now came expansion and deceleration. On the walls of light that swirled around him played a cine film of his sixty-three years. He saw his beloved Lillian, Nicholas and Alex, his parents. First love. First sex. First loving sex. The perennial mysteries of birth, marriage and death.

He was in each scene and out of it. An observer and a player. And not just a player of himself. Here was Gina, whose heart he'd broken when he was seventeen. Now he knew her pain from the inside. Five year old Alex squealed when he wasn't allowed a new toy. Ernest wept with him.

But it wasn't all bad. There were the great moments as well. When he told Patterson that he had the promotion, Ernest felt the joy swell within him. And there was the satisfaction of knowing that the child he'd sponsored in Africa – Mikele – had made something of his life by becoming a doctor.

It came to an end in seconds. Ernest was once more peaceful. But it was more than that. He was also cleansed. His life was sloughed off, showered away. He'd seen and understood and now he expanded again. He was becoming infinite.

Ernest saw a new light stretching down to him, so that he was neither pulled nor pushed, yearning nor reaching.

Now he was embraced.

Penrhys was on the verge of giving up. Six minutes became seven. He looked at his colleagues on the crash team, hoping desperately that someone else would make the call. They lowered their eyes to avoid his gaze. They all knew it was his responsibility. He sighed. Then Penrhys gripped the paddles of the defibrillator and called again for the charge.

He plunged. The body jolted and jumped and the beep they had all been hoping for came, first slow and then quickening, urgent and temporal. The nurses exchanged relieved smiles.

Someone was forcing him out of that embrace. They caught Ernest's heels and pulled him down. The life of union dissolved into separation. Eternal contentment became eternal restlessness as he returned to that room. To that body.

It was a rewind, with the same discordant jumble of sounds and images. Except there was real violence as he plummeted, dive-bombing back into that lump of clay. Impact was misery. Pain consumed him and the trap closed back over him, sealing him into his fleshy tomb.

The doctors were stunned by Ernest's recovery. Lillian put it down to private care and was grateful. She'd been too upset to know how long he'd been dead. The fact was horrific enough. Yet there was still an allure to it, however much she tried to deny it. A childish need that pulsed in her heart. Her husband had visited with Death and Death had sent him back to her.

Mr Holman was eager to discharge his patient. His impatience began with Ernest's return to consciousness. For two days, he lay suspended in sleep. Then he awoke peacefully, but full of stories of what 'had happened' in theatre.

'Don't upset yourself, Ernest.'

'I'm not upset. I'm indescribably happy. I know where I'm going when I die.'

Holman smiled benignly, 'It's a normal effect, as death approaches. A rush of endorphins. For everyone's sake, it would be best if you forgot all about it.' He stared at Ernest, as if he was a wilful child.

'Yes, Mr Holman. Whatever you say.'

Mr Holman smiled with relief. It really didn't do to give credence to such illusions.

Discharge day came. It was an indescribable joy to Lillian that Ernest was hers again.

Recovery was a long slow process. Nicholas and Alex suggested a nurse, but Lillian shooed the idea away. There was a manual and medication. She was his wife after all. She wanted no strangers interfering.

The pride was all hers when she took him for his first walk around the garden. Together they admired dark-eyed pansies, lily trumpets and the purple plumage of a Japanese maple. This had always been her domain and Ernest was proud of what she had achieved. He praised her with soft noises of delight. His spirit, however, was hollow. Untouched. Ernest dug his thumbnails into his palms, hoping to feel.

When would his lust for life return? When would he stop wishing and be grateful for the second chance the light had given him? He kept his own counsel, not wishing to seem ungrateful or strange.

But, try as he might to get on with life, Ernest's eyes dulled. His hair went unwashed. The silver stubble on his chin thickened into a beard.

Lillian was worried. Mr Holman had mentioned the possibility of depression after major surgery, but she had dismissed it. Ernest had never known depression in his life.

Now he grieved incessantly. The wounds of his body might be healed, but there seemed to be a deep wound of longing in their place. Every time she tried to immerse him in the mundane, the stuff of living, Lillian felt a hot knife pierce her. He grew tired and irritated so quickly. She kept telling herself it was the after-effects of his trauma. But it was more than that. It was an enemy she couldn't fight, because she didn't know what it was.

Lillian wrung her hands when he asked to go to church. It had never been their sort of thing. She wondered what it could mean.

Ernest saw the worry in his wife's eyes, the constant question in her furrowed brow.

'Why are you changed?'

He wanted to tell her, but it was locked within his chest. The world was a permanent winter. Not even her solicitous love could anchor him. Church was a last resort, a hope that the veil would be lifted just an inch. That a crumb of vision might fall to him. Anything to sustain him in the awful indefinite hours until he could welcome death again.

They returned worse than ever. She was closed up and resentful, embarrassed at appearing so suddenly in front of the regular congregants.

Ernest raged. He felt nothing other than oppression. He took his place among the stony-faced worshippers, but knew he was so very different.

They believed. He knew.

Lillian went out into the garden to weep. She raised her head to the sky and prayed silently that she might understand what was going on. Then, her heart pounding, she went inside the house to find him. It was time to know.

He rose to embrace her, clinging to her slight body in the hope that she would save him from drowning. Then they sank down into the sofa, like children whispering their secrets, her spotted hand clasped in his.

They both cried. Lillian was sliced up by his words.

'It was so utterly beautiful... it burns within me at every moment... I can't see anything in this world but compare it to that one... I want to go back.'

She wanted to scream, to beat at his chest, to tear his heart into pieces in revenge.

'What about me?'

But when Lillian tried to articulate it, it caught in the back of her throat and she spent the next few days trying to swallow it away.

Ernest was a little lighter, a little freer after their talk. Lillian resented that and he knew that she'd heard in his words an unintended rejection.

158

As if he could be tired of her!

He sipped a glass of red wine in the conservatory and felt calm spread over his tired limbs. She needed time to adjust to the idea. Particularly his request. But she would help. He knew that. A lifetime together guaranteed that. It lent them both extraordinary powers of loyalty.

Lillian resisted initially. She would fight for her husband, distract him from these shadows, these half-remembrances. She would re-kindle the fire in him. Galvanised, she wiped her eyes and went up to the attic.

'What are you doing?'

'Just fetching the photo albums.'

They passed the night with them. She would not turn the page until they recalled every single paperbound moment, each faded occasion, each distant face. They laughed, they cried, they scratched their heads and trawled across the years, revisiting each corner of their married life.

At midnight, Ernest's eyes were dry and heavy. She led him up to bed as if he were her child. He smiled sleepily and kissed her, calling her 'Kitten'.

'It was good to remember all those years, Lillian.'

'Wasn't it?'

He kissed her goodnight and fell straight to sleep.

Lillian lay beside him, her body rigid. She was forging a battle plan, working it over until tempered and faultless. She rose with the dawn, hopeful at last. She woke Ernest after her first phone call of the day. Nicholas, their eldest, agreed to come over with his sons. He would be here after lunch.

'That's sudden.' Ernest scratched his head, still fuzzy from the previous night.

'Well, it's half term and the boys are off. And besides...'

'Besides what?'

'No one knows how long we've got left, do we?'

Ernest winced.

For the next fortnight, she campaigned as hard as possible. Each day there were phone calls and visits, memories to be cracked open and savoured. Alex sent parcels of letters and photographs, updating them both on his own family.

Ernest graciously received this attention. He knew what she was doing. Poor girl! She was so afraid of what he longed for. If only he could reassure her. But the subject was closed between them. And the more she forced him to acknowledge the blessings of his life, the more Ernest hungered for eternal joy.

Until he could stand it no longer. He was the rope in a tug-of-war between Lillian and the hereafter. She was a coiled spring, full of the will to make him stay.

In a quiet moment, over a bite of lunch between trips, he decided to tell her.

'Lillian, we need to talk. I know what you're doing and it won't work.'

She sprang up from the table, eyes downcast, full of tears.

'I don't know what you mean, dearest. Finish up! George and Diane will be here in a moment... I've had enough,' she laughed coldly. 'I'm watching my figure.' She made to leave the room, but turned back to say, 'I won't hear any more of this talk Ernest. You are not leaving me...'

'It's for the best. We can't go on like this. I'll end up hating you.'

His words unwound her. She rubbed her face, stretching the skin and pinching it, hiding her tears. Then she approached him, took his face into her hands and stared into his soul.

'My beloved. How can I help you?'

It was a simple plan. A bottle of painkillers washed down with a good single malt. Then, just to be sure, she would hold a pillow to his face. It was so gentle that Lillian could not wash the taste of brutality out of her mouth.

As the day approached, they found their conversation drying up, though the urgency to speak did not. They began to talk through touch, through looks, through passionate kisses. Still, he was slipping through her fingers...

They chose a warm and glowing day. Sunset – Ernest's favourite hour. On the CD player, Ella Fitzgerald sang *Someone To Watch Over Me*. Lillian poured him a full tumbler of whisky and placed it on the table by the bed. Next to it, she positioned the small plastic bottle, so utilitarian and innocuous. She shook as she gave him the first pills. His hand grasped awkwardly. Damn his throat, that it should tighten now, when he

161

needed this to be as quick as possible.

Watching him was a mixture of the unreal and the terrifying. The sun died behind them as she held his head, cradling him as his eyes rolled and his breathing slowed. When he was unconscious, she laid him down, took the pillow and pressed it over his face, afraid to exert any pressure in case she hurt him.

Pull yourself together Lillian, she thought. She pressed harder, looking down to see his breath ebbing and then ceasing. Lillian dropped the pillow and sank to the floor, rocking back and forth, trembling.

Don't Try This at Home

There's a gap in the fence, right at the bottom of the schoolyard. Dad pokes his head through and waves at Joe, who takes a look round to check he isn't spotted before he joins him.

Dad hugs him. 'Hiya, Joe.'

'Hiya, Dad.'

Madeleine is in the passenger seat of Dad's Cortina. She waves to Joe, who waves back. She's pretty, not at all like Mum, who cut off her hair last year so that, from the back, she looks a bit like a man. Joe pushes away thoughts of Mum and what she'd say if she knew what they were up to. But it's his day. He's waited yonks for the film to come out. And Dad promised he would take him to the very first showing.

Joe kisses Madeleine on the cheek and sets his satchel on the back seat. Dad explains that he phoned the school secretary and said that Joe had a last minute dental appointment.

'Thanks Dad.' Joe knows he isn't really supposed to thank adults for lying. But they do it all the time. And this lie's for his own good.

Because it's an afternoon, the cinema isn't crowded. Madeleine insists on getting Joe his own mint chocolate Cornetto. Dad tells him not to wolf it down in one go, otherwise he'll be sick. Joe pushes his luck and asks for a Pepsi. Dad buys him the smallest size and holds onto it until the Cornetto is finished.

There are tonnes and tonnes of trailers. Mostly little kid films. Joe tries not to watch, because he has sophisticated tastes. He reaches out for his Pepsi and sees Dad is holding Madeleine's hand. Joe can't imagine wanting to hold hands with a girl. Dad says it'll happen, one day.

At least Dad smiles when he's with Madeleine. Joe can't remember the days when Dad and Mum smiled at each other or held hands.

Finally, the film appears. For the next couple of hours, Joe isn't aware of anything but Superman.

Coming back to real life is like being woken from the best dream ever. Joe falls sullen and silent, even refusing to kiss Madeleine when they drop her off at her house.

'Joe?'

'Hm?'

'Whatever Mum says, will you tell her it was just us two today? Please?'

Joe's used to covering up for Dad. Madeleine is their little secret.

'And, Son?'

'Yes?'

'No matter what happens, remember that I love you.'

Joe smiles. Inside, though, he's feeling really sick. The Pepsi is bubbling up in his stomach .

They pull up and Mum is waiting, leaning against the front wall of their house, arms

164

wrapped around her waist. Her face is blank, but Joe knows this won't last. Sometimes he hates her.

Dad gets out of the car and hangs back for Joe. 'Here we are,' he says to Jan, who grimaces in response.

Dad turns back to him and lowers his voice. 'Come on, Son. Time to face the music.'

Joe unbuckles his seatbelt, aware that his stomach has slipped down into his shoes. He looks up, hoping that Superman might be on his way to rescue him from the almighty fight that he knows is going to happen, but the sky is empty. All Joe can feel is the heat of Mum's anger.

Dad steers him up the drive. Joe does his best to pass his mum and step straight into the shadowy mouth of the hall. Jan reaches out and takes hold of his arm. She gives him the X-ray look.

'Had a nice time, Tiger?'

There is no appeasing answer, so Joe tells her the truth. 'Yes, thank you Mum.' He doesn't add, 'Until we had to come home.'

'Go on up to your room, Joseph. Your father and I need to talk.'

He obeys, trudging across to the stairs. Halfway up, Joe stops and glances over his shoulder, to offer Dad an encouraging smile. Stand firm, Dad, he wants to say.

But the approaching storm crackles over his skin. He hopes that Mum won't start outside, that she'll deny the neighbours ringside seats to this latest battle.

The landing is a huge black void, except for the old wardrobe by Joe's bedroom door. Once, he and a friend climbed into it. But they found no fur coats, no fauns, no magical land. Just pungent mothballs and rough pine backboard that held firm beneath the pressure of disappointed fingers.

He's moved on from Narnia. Now he's a super-hero.

An unexpected shaft of sunlight strikes the window, bleaching Joe's room. He blinks furiously as his eyes adjust.

Slung over his bed is the red canvas. It used to be part of his play tent, but now it serves a greater purpose. No superhero can fly without his cape.

Joe snatches up the canvas and drapes it around his shoulders, examining himself in the mirror. He looks more and more like his real self every day. All he needs now is Dad's Brylcreem and his own red Wellingtons from downstairs.

This means that Joe has to face that landing again. He takes a deep breath and closes his eyes, recalling the point in the film where Clark fights evil Superman. Rising repeatedly, though the onslaught keeps coming and everything seems doomed, Clark wins through.

Taking courage at this, Joe resists the thump-ing of his heart and the panic commanding his legs. He thrusts his shoulders back and raises his head, striding across to the stairs and descending, resisting the urge to look back, in case the dark-ness monsters bare their teeth at him and mock his bravado.

The argument is in full flow. Dad stammers in Clark Kent fashion. Mum wails and shrieks. Something thuds against a wall.

'Jesus, Jan. Calm down.'

'CALM DOWN? CALM DOWN? If you hadn't kidnapped my son, I'd be fine. He should have been in school. How can you be so irresponsible?'

'It's one afternoon off, Jan. He's eight. How much damage is one afternoon off going to do him?'

Silence. Though he's tired of their rows, Joe can't resist eavesdropping. And it's about him, for a change.

'He needed to get out, Jan. We needed to get out, Jan. Just because you want to bury yourself in here, waiting for nuclear meltdown, doesn't mean we all have to.'

'You took him to the cinema? Filled his head with tripe?'

Jan's venom pierces Joe. Tripe? If she would only sit down to watch... She would know that everything will be alright. That Superman can save the world.

He can't listen to any more. He pads through the kitchen, past the larder piled floor to ceiling with cans of food. Cling peaches, stewed steak, and vegetable medley. Mum's planned it so that, if World War Three breaks out, they have a balanced meal every day for four years. She's stashed tin openers all round the house, taking every precaution she can against starvation. When the

167

time comes, they'll transport all of this down to the bunker she's built at the bottom of the garden.

By the back door, next to Dad's steel-toed boots and his rickety bicycle, sit Joe's Wellingtons. He slips off his tennis shoes, and pulls on the boots, wincing at their cold insides.

Jeans will do for trousers. But Dad's got some red satin shorts that he can wear over them and then there's Joe's most treasured possession – his genuine Superman jumper – a gift from Madeleine.

Joe squeaks past the living room door. Silence again. He can't decide if this is more worrying than when Mum and Dad scream at each other, when Dad threatens to get the doctor to take Mum away.

Don't think about it, he tells himself. It'll be over soon. He pictures this house, empty except for Mum, a tearful wraith wondering what she did wrong. He feels sorry for her, but then remembers that she called the film tripe. Last week she ripped down Joe's posters. He came home from school to find a bedroom of bare woodchip, bright pitted rectangles where all the images of his hero once hung.

Why does someone so unhappy want everyone else to feel the same way? He can't figure it out. All Joe wants is a cuddle. A pair of strong arms around him. He often climbs up into Dad's arms when they have a moment alone. But Dad's cuddles would be nothing to one from Superman. Joe allows himself a moment to imagine this.

'Was SHE there?'

The next offensive begins in the living room. Joe takes a deep breath and launches off to complete his quest.

In his parents' bedroom, Joe inhales Mum's sweet and flowery perfume. The quilt is pulled down. Dad's side of the bed is smooth and undisturbed. There are mascara tracks staining Mum's pillow. Joe wakes most nights and listens to her sobbing. In the mornings, Joe meets Dad as he emerges from the spare room.

He's not usually allowed in here. But they're too busy tearing each other apart to notice. And he's only borrowing one pair of shorts. Dad won't mind.

Joe pulls open a drawer. He giggles when he sees Mum's bras. They're so foreign and mysterious. Unnecessarily complicated, with all that lace and embroidery attempting to disguise the unyielding scaffolding. And those little hooks that you have to fasten behind your back.

He doesn't understand why she bothers. She could easily get away with wearing a vest, like him. But, apparently, she has to have them to preserve her femininity. Joe wishes she would grow her hair back to the way it was before she went to Greenham Common the first time. When she looked a bit like Farrah Fawcett.

Dad's stuff isn't in this drawer. Joe tries the next one down. He clears a pile of shapeless y-fronts and discovers Dad's magazines. The ones Mum says degrade women. Joe glimpses a nipple, a string of pearls tight around a slender pale neck. His eyes travel down to the dark triangle of wiry hair. It turns his stomach. But he's also hot and excited. His palms are clammy.

He can't bring himself to take the magazine out of the drawer. That X-ray vision of Mum's will catch him out. She'll be so disappointed.

Joe turns away, grabs the shorts and slams the drawer shut.

Only the Brylcreem to collect and then Joe is back in his own room. He retrieves a shoebox from under his bed. This is the hidden shrine – the photos Mum doesn't know about it. There's some of Superman, but also of Dad and Madeleine, taken last summer when the Cortina was broken and Madeleine drove them to places instead. One time they went to the Planetarium. Another day was Chester Zoo, where an orang-utan took a liking to Dad and Madeleine covered Joe's eyes with her hand, laughing all the while. Mum stayed at home, busy with her survival plan.

When the photos were developed, Dad asked Joe to look after them and not mention them to Mum. Despite Madeleine's kindness, Mum doesn't like her. Joe doesn't understand it. It seems that some adults, his Mum included, enjoy not being friends with people.

Joe puts the Madeleine photos to one side and carefully draws out the Holy Grail. A signed photo that Madeleine got him from America. Superman, arms folded across his chest, cape ruffled by the breeze. This is everything Joe aspires to be.

He sets the precious photo on his dressing table and kneels before it briefly. Then Joe rises, slips off his wellies and slides the shorts over his legs. They're too big, but he secures them with his snake belt. He takes the sweatshirt out of a drawer and pulls it on. The boots go back on and then Joe opens the Brylcreem.

He scoops up some of the cold, greasy muck and squelches it through his hair. Then he drags a comb through his matted strands and slowly sculpts a DA from his floppy fringe.

He thinks about how proud they'll both be when they realize their son is a superhero. He can't, obviously, be Superman, so Joe is Superboy. Once his powers are completely under his control, Joe will sort out the adults' mess. He'll start with Mum and Dad and then he'll convince Mr Reagan that nuking Russia wouldn't be a good idea. He'll get everyone to be friends with Mrs Thatcher.

The crash of the living room door shatters Joe's train of thought. Dad stomps up the stairs, with Mum calling after him.

'That's right. Run away. You have to give me an answer sooner or later, Brian. I have to know.'

At this point, Dad usually slams the spare bedroom door and turns his record player up, so that the house is filled with Frank Sinatra or Supertramp, depending on how bad the argument is.

Joe holds his breath and waits. There's a tap on his door. Dad sticks his head round and flashes Joe an unconvincing smile.

'What are you doing, Joe-Joe?'

He can't help but cringe. He used to love this name, but that was before he became a hero. Once upon a time, Dad was his hero. Now he's a sad man with greying hair and sagging chin, the skin around his pale eyes red and tender.

'You look great, Son.'

'Thanks.'

'Are those my pants?' Dad points to the satin shorts.

'Yes. I... I... borrowed them. Sorry.'

Dad shrugs. Joe breathes a sigh of relief.

'It doesn't matter. Listen, Joseph, there's something I need to explain to you.'

Dad sits himself on the edge of the bed. He picks up one of the photos and smiles.

'It's okay Dad. I understand.'

Dad folds his arms behind his head, sighs deeply and leans back. There's mud in the tread of his left shoe.

'I'm sorry, Joe-Joe.'

Joe turns away from the mirror and crosses to the bed. His cape slides away and pools across the floor. Sinking down, Joe lays his head on Dad's chest. They don't speak for a minute or two. Joe listens to their synchronised breathing. Affection rushes out of him and covers Dad's denim shirt with tears.

Dad strokes his back. 'Come on. Things will get better. I promise.'

'Joseph?' Dad shifts so that he can look Joe in the face. 'Madeleine's going to have a baby. I have to... go be with her.'

Joe stares at him blankly. He wasn't expecting this.

'But I want you to come as well. So does Madeleine. I know it's a big change. But you'll see your mother at weekends. And you always wanted a brother or sister.'

Joe is so surprised by Dad's speech that he leaps up. He catches sight of himself in the mirror. Just a kid in wellies, wearing his Dad's pants over his jeans. He's really nothing without the cape.

The door flies open. Mum stands there, full of thunder.

'What's this?'

Dad jumps up, blocking Mum's way. 'Jan, I was just talking with Joe.'

'Telling him more of your lies? Arranging to kidnap him from school again? Filling his head with nonsense about how his Mum's going crazy?'

'Jan...'

Mum elbows Dad in the ribs. He falls onto the bed and photos scatter like confetti. She's down on her hands and knees examining them before either Joe or his Dad can stop her. Joe knows that this is very bad, but the look of pure hatred on his mother's face freezes his blood.

'At last,' she says, in little more than a whisper, 'the truth.'

Why hasn't she turned her X-ray vision on Dad before now?

Dad shrugs. 'Yes, Jan. Madeleine's carrying my

baby. So I'm leaving you. But Joe's coming with me.'

'WHAT?'

Mum's scream is horrible.

'You can't take him. What if the four minute warning sounds? He needs to be in the shelter with me!'

Joe snatches up his cape and secures it firmly round his neck. This is a job for Superboy.

'Jan! PLEASE STOP IT.'

'You bastard! You're not taking him away.'

Joe tries to speak but Dad drowns him out. 'Don't call me that in front of my son.'

'If you try and leave with him, Brian... I'll call the police. I'll make sure they know what an irresponsible parent you are, making him skip school and forcing him to live in a dream world.'

They're squaring up to each other now, screaming into each other's faces. Joe tries to intervene, pulling on Mum's leg.

'Mum, let go of Dad, please.'

She doesn't answer. Instead she tries to shrug Joe off. The cape slips and Joe loses his footing. He hears the crack as his head slams into the bedroom door. Then a moment of silence, really precious silence, before more screaming.

'JOE!'

Mum and Dad both cry for his attention, but he slips out of their grasp, lighter than air. He ascends, watching his screaming parents shrink to dots of anger. For once, Joe's cape isn't strangling him or threatening to slip off. It streams out behind him, a pennant of heroism.

'Will I see them again,' Joe asks Superman, who is waiting for him somewhere above the clouds.

Superman smiles. 'Let's leave the adults to it, kid. We've got us some saving the world to do.'

Acknowledgements

My thanks go to:

Paul and Stu at Tonto Books, for championing new writers (including myself) and contributing to the renaissance of the short story.

Laura Hird, for her patience, wise advice and enthusiasm. It's been a privilege to learn from someone who has mastered the form.

Rosalind Wyllie, who has been there throughout the process, offering encouragement whenever my self-belief failed.

Much missed Chrissie Glazebrook, who encouraged me when I was ready to give up and whose wicked humour, I hope, shines through in these tales.

Claire Malcolm and New Writing North for all the support and opportunities they have offered to develop my writing career.

Friends (and strangers) who read the embryonic forms of some of these stories and offered criticism, advice or a simple 'I enjoyed it'.

David Steele, for keeping my feet on the ground.

My family, for being my bedrock.

If you feel that you haven't been fully acknowledged, you can complain at:
http://leavingtheroomwithdignity.blogspot.com/

About the author

Stephen Shieber was born in Germany in 1975.
He now lives and works in Newcastle upon Tyne.
As a child he wanted to be either Flash Gordon or
Buck Rogers. When he grew up, he wanted to be a
contemplative monk. He now teaches Religious
Studies because he never quite made it to the
English teaching course.

Stephen has a pathological fear of cling peaches
and is one of the few people he knows who has
visited Finland. Although he develops vertigo on
the second rung of a stepladder, Stephen harbours
a secret desire to experience free-fall sky diving. If
he ever comes to power, he will imprison parents
who give their children ridiculous and embarrass-
ing names.

This is his first collection of short stories.

READ MORE FROM TONTO BOOKS:

Everything You Ever Wanted
A novel by Rosalind Wyllie
Paperback, £7.99, 9780955632631, available now

'I'm every woman they have ever dreamt of. I'll do anything –
I'll do things they didn't even know they wanted.'

Tiggy's stuck in a rut – trapped in a half-life as a stripper at
a Mayfair club, surviving on dope and vodka, and desperate
for her married lover to leave his wife.

Scarlett is different – she's more confident, stunningly
beautiful, and willing to do absolutely anything to get exactly
what she wants.

Tiggy is intoxicated by the enigmatic Scarlett, following her
into an arousing world of sex and excitement. But Scarlett
has her own agenda, and she doesn't do anything for free.
Sooner or later Tiggy's going to have to pay.

Evocatively set in the summer of 1991, *Everything You Ever
Wanted* is a smart and gritty tale of two young women's
colourful adventures in a London sex industry where money
talks, and boundaries are there to be broken.

*'A sharp and stunning debut. Taut prose, original voice,
visuals that crackle and shock. Wyllie trips the reader into a
foreboding world where sex sells and friendships are dubious.'*
– Caroline Smailes

*'Sharp, witty and unnervingly streetwise, Wyllie is a name
you're going to hear more of.'* – Carol Clewlow

READ MORE FROM TONTO BOOKS:

9987
A novel by Nik Jones
Paperback, £7.99, 9780955632662, available in January 2009

To him, the shop is everything; always neat and tidy, safe and reliable. The rental DVDs carefully categorised, alphabetised and memorised. But when one valued member starts to leave bloodstains on the fresh new carpet, handing back porn still sticky with gore and paying in smeared with rusting red, his careful existence is compromised and uncomfortable.
Then the girl arrives with her pale skin, green eyes and fresh scarlet slashed beneath her thin cotton blouse. He wants to rescue and protect her. He wants to be with her. Forever.

Tragic and dark, 9987 is a story about a wholly jagged and at times disturbing, uncaring world where only three things are constant: fantasy, loneliness and love. A tale about a crime that only one person seems to care about.

READ MORE FROM TONTO BOOKS:

Make It Back
A novel by Sarah Shaw
Paperback, £7.99, 9780955632679, available in January 2009

Why would a loving mother abandon her child? In Make It Back, Muriel leaves her family to nurse sick and injured children in the Spanish Civil War. Forty years later, Muriel's decision leads her granddaughter, Dee, into love, into danger and, finally, into the passion and dust of south-eastern Spain.